THE SILVER CHALICE

For Jake

ABOUT THE AUTHOR

Shelagh Jones was born in London of Irish-Scottish parentage. She is the author of two books for children, *Save the Unicorns* and *The DerrynaLushca Dragon*, previously published by The Children's Press. Having worked as a drama teacher for many years, she has a great deal of experience with children and enjoys directing plays. She now lives in Co. Wicklow with her husband and assorted animals and has one grown-up daughter.

ABOUT THE ILLUSTRATOR

Nicky Hooper graduated in illustration and design from the College of Marketing and Design in 1994. Since then she has worked as a freelance illustrator and her work has appeared in many Irish publications. She lives and works in Dublin.

THE
SILVER CHALICE

SHELAGH JONES

ILLUSTRATED BY NICKY HOOPER

WOLFHOUND PRESS

First published 1996 by
WOLFHOUND PRESS Ltd
68 Mountjoy Square
Dublin 1

© 1996 Shelagh Jones
Illustrations © Nicky Hooper

This book is fiction. All characters, incidents and names have no connection with any person living or dead. Any apparent resemblance is purely coincidental.

Wolfhound Press receives financial assistance from the Arts Council/An Chomhairle Ealaíon, Dublin.

British Library Cataloguing in Publication Data
A catalogue record for this book is available from the British Library.

ISBN 0 86327 540 0

Typesetting: Wolfhound Press
Cover illustration and design: Nicky Hooper
Printed in the UK by Cox & Wyman Ltd., Reading, Berks.

CONTENTS

CHAPTER 1
THE FACE IN THE GLASS

'You should not boast,' Paul was to say to himself. 'You should not boast. Look what happens!'

Paul stared at his face in the museum showcase. He had been standing there some time, trying to avoid the rest of the class. It was his own fault, and he knew it.

The town where Paul went to school was not very big, but it boasted a market square, three churches, seven pubs, two supermarkets, a library, and a museum. The museum was not very big either, but thanks to the fact that Paul's grandfather was an archaeologist, there were a good many interesting things in it.

Paul was very proud of his grandfather. Usually, there was nothing Paul liked better than to wander round the glass cases in the museum, gloating over the objects on display, reminding himself that there was a 'family connection' because his grandfather had dug them up.

On the particular day when this story begins, however, Paul was *not* enjoying himself. It was the class outing. Mr. O'Mahony the history teacher had decided they should down their pencils and rubbers, leave their dog-eared, biro-marked books, and as he put it, 'Go out into the Community'.

Whatever else the 'Community' might be, with Mr. O'Mahony it started at the museum. As the minutes of the old clock on the wall ticked slowly by and Mr.

O'Mahony's voice droned on and on, Paul began to feel that not only did the Community start at the museum, it ended there as well. He cringed whenever Mr. O'Mahony mentioned Professor Sheean's name – Professor Sheean was his grandfather. How he wished he had never boasted of the fact in earlier conversations! Each time Mr. O'Mahony pointed out a gold torque, or a jewelled reliquary, or a Viking helmet, or an Iron Age spear, drawing breath for yet another lecture, Paul could feel twenty pairs of eyes turned accusingly in *his* direction. 'This is *your* fault,' the eyes seemed to be saying. At last, unable to bear the feeling of guilt (even if two generations removed) another second, Paul had left the class poring over a case of Bronze Age pottery, and slunk to the far end of the room. Even here, he could not escape notice!

'Well, Paul! Come to have a look at the chalice?' The cheerful voice – *much* too loud, Paul thought! – belonged to Liam, the curator. He and Paul were old friends. Many a happy afternoon had they spent together in the past, discussing the use of this object, the date of that, and recalling the day when Professor Sheean had discovered it. Today, with the class sniggering only a few yards away, Paul was in no mood to be sociable. He turned his back , pretending not to hear, and gazed fixedly into the glass case which held the chalice.

Of all the pieces in the museum, the Kilcarrigan Chalice was undoubtedly Paul's favourite. It was not so large, nor so fine as the chalices he had seen in the National Museum in Dublin. Nevertheless, it was very beautiful and the pride of Grandfather's collection. After it was found it had to be sent away for expert polishing and restoration. Now, it stood – almost perfect except for a tiny dent the restorers had failed to remove – in a pool of floodlight, in a showcase of its own. It had broad flat handles like ears, delicately embossed with curling spirals which seemed to have no beginning and no end. A band of starry crystals crowned its lip. Amongst the crystals were pieces of dark blue enamel, like chips from a midnight sky. One of the pieces was missing. Paul liked to imagine that the Abbot of Kilcarrigan had sucked too hard one day, while taking the wine, and had swallowed it. He wondered if it had given the good man a stomach ache. A second row of crystals circled the foot of the chalice. These were interspersed by exotic yellow stones with brown stripes, which Grandfather had told Paul were known as 'Tiger's Eyes'. Like the great cat's eyes they kept their secrets, seeming to watch the modern world with a mysterious clouded stealth.

A mystery surrounded the finding of the Kilcarrigan Chalice. Grandfather had not found it amongst the other objects within the abbey ruins – stonemasons' tools, broken pots from the kitchen, a wooden rake, parts of a plough, useful everyday things, showing that the brothers were busy, practical fellows when not at prayer. He had come upon it quite by chance, while taking a walk by the river several miles downstream. He had tripped over it, in fact, half buried in the river bank.

It must have been there for centuries, Paul supposed, so why had nobody tripped over it before? What was it doing there so far from the abbey walls? Had it been stolen? Lost on a journey? Dropped from a boat? There was no way of knowing. Sighing, he withdrew his eyes from his own reflection, and leaning his elbows against the wooden frame of the case rested his chin on his hands, and studied the chalice.

He had not been standing this way many minutes when he became aware that someone else was looking at the chalice. It was not Liam. He had moved away to sweep the floor. It was not one of the boys, for they were all clustered around Mr. O'Mahony, being treated to a talk on Bronze Age settlements. Glancing up, Paul saw there were now *two* faces reflected in the glass.

The first face was his own. Sandy hair standing up on end because he would push it with his fingers, glasses halfway down his nose, tie askew (in later years people would say that Paul was exactly like his grandfather, but of course he did not know that yet). The second face was that of a stranger.

It was not an unpleasant face, although it had a pimple on its chin, so Paul did not know why he should give a little shudder. It was round and smooth as a baby's, with plump cheeks and a snub nose, framed by a fringe of black hair above which rose the rest of the head, bald and peaked like an egg. The babyish look was emphasised by the fact that the little man (he was not much taller than Paul) possessed a pair of the largest bluest eyes the boy had ever seen. To his shock and confusion, he noticed that these eyes were brimming with tears.

It was too late to move away, the man was standing right behind him. Embarrassed, he pretended once more to study the chalice, hoping his emotional companion would move on to the next case. It seemed he had no intention of doing so. Every time Paul glanced up, he was still there, tears pouring down his face.

THE

K I L C A R R I g a N

C H a L I C E

SIX th   C E N T UR y

'Bother!' thought Paul. 'This can't go on.' He turned round sharply .... Imagine his amazement when he saw that there was no one there!

There was no time to investigate. The class was advancing, headed by Mr. O'Mahony, old tweed coat flapping round his long lean body like a pair of shabby wings. Soon Paul was crushed against the showcase with 'Fatty' O'Rourke breathing in his ear.

'The Kilcarrigan Chalice,' Mr. O'Mahony was intoning, 'is all that is left of the vast treasure of Kilcarrigan Abbey, which stood by the river some five miles away from here. In the year 836 – make a note of the date, boys – the Vikings, or as they were known in those days, 'the Lochlannachs', led by Ulfberht Longarm, sailed up the river plundering and setting fire to the abbey and putting all its occupants to the sword. The riches of the abbey were lost. No one knows what became of them. It could be they were divided between the robbers and taken back to Scandinavia, to grace their long halls; it could be they went down with the ships in a gale, for there is no record of Ulfberht ever reaching home .... It was quite by chance that Professor Arthur Sheean should come upon this beautiful chalice, half-buried in the river bank.'

'You see! He's a chancer,' smirked O'Rourke, nudging Paul. For such a fat boy he had remarkably sharp elbows!

Paul began to make a rude face at Fatty through the glass, and stopped .... The little man was there again – wedged between Fatty and Stephen Sullivan, who was engaged in an elaborate conversation in mime with Francis Tierney standing next to him.

Mr. O'Mahony chanted on. Nobody was paying attention, least of all Paul. He was watching the stranger in the glass.

He could see now he was a member of a Holy Order, thus accounting for the bald patch on his head. There was a brown hood lying in crumpled folds upon his shoulders. Whenever he raised his hand to wipe a tear – an action he performed frequently – Paul caught sight of the wide, coarsely woven sleeve of a monk's habit. It seemed he was no happier than before. His plump cheeks were wet and shiny, so was his nose. He sniffed repeatedly.

What Paul could not understand was that, although the little man was wedged in by the crowd of children, those all around seemed not to see him. There was James Murphy aiming a paper pellet at Michael Flynn, regardless of the fact that the monk stood in between. Francis Tierney was talking right through him to Dermot Whyte on the other side.

'Would you like a look at the chalice out of its case?' Liam had approached, beaming with pleasure at the chance of showing off his finest treasure. Without waiting for an answer he produced a heavy bunch of keys. They rattled as he applied one to the lock. Lifting the chalice with extreme care, he passed it over the boys' heads to Mr. O'Mahony.

What happened next baffled everyone, but Paul.

A hand reached up. Snatched the chalice. And disappeared.

'Which of you boys did *that*?' Mr. O'Mahony towered above them like a shabby bird of prey. 'Not a boy moves until I find the culprit.' – An unnecessary order: they were all rooted to the spot! – 'Come now, I distinctly saw a hand and a brown sleeve' (which told him nothing, for they were all wearing brown blazers). 'Who has the chalice? Francis Tierney! You seem smitten with a desire to laugh. Do you know something about this? Seamus Friel! What have you hidden behind your back?'

It took a long time for each boy to be questioned, and for the museum to be searched (Liam was in a state of shock. 'What will the Professor say?' he kept repeating). Quite long enough, Paul thought, to allow a light-footed, light-fingered gentleman in Holy Orders to slip outside and get away. It was a very subdued class that eventuallystepped into the street. They were told to go home. Mr. O'Mahony and Liam hurried off in distress to report the matter to the guards.

'I'm starving. Do you want some crisps? Shall we go to the shops?'

'No thanks.' Paul looked with distaste at Fatty's flabby features. He himself enjoyed eating, but really Fatty never stopped! Besides, he had something on his mind. 'I'll miss my bus,' he lied.

The bus came early and he climbed aboard. Feeling tense – unable to relax – he did not move down to the back as usual to make a note of the registration numbers of the following cars, but chose a seat at the front. They had not gone far when he saw what he was looking for .... A small monk in a brown habit hustling along the street, his rope girdle flying behind, his sandals flip-flapping on the pavement like the webbed feet of a duck. He had pulled his hood up so that his face was hidden, but Paul knew instinctively it was the same man he had seen in the museum. He was carrying a parcel!

In an instant, Paul was on his feet and had leant on the bell press. He was out of the bus before it could stop. The monk must have sensed that he was being followed, for he began to run. It was market day and the streets were crowded. Paul kept bumping into people as he zig-zagged along the pavement, trying to keep the little man in view. He almost lost him when he got mixed up in a flock of sheep. The monk just floated through the pack of woolly bodies without difficulty. The shepherd ignored him, but a lean collie raised her hackles and growled suspiciously. When at last the boy caught up, the monk was heading for the square.

'Drat!' thought Paul. 'If he gets among the stalls I'll never find him.' He quickened his pace.

To his relief, the man turned sharp right up a blind alley. 'Now I have him!' Paul thought. He was hot on the monk's heels as he dodged round the corner and slid to a stop.

After the noise and bustle of the street the alley was silent and dim – and empty!

The little monk was nowhere to be seen.

CHAPTER 2
THE PARCEL

There was only one other way out of the alley, and that was through a side door into the church. Except when a service was being held it was always kept locked. As Paul approached, however, he could hear the muffled rhythmic murmur of people at prayer. Timidly, he tried the handle. The door creaked open and he slipped inside.

He had hoped to avoid being noticed, but in the gloom his foot caught on a hassock and he fell clumsily against a tall candle-holder. To his dismay Father Finnegan paused in the very act of raising the Host, peering with mild reproach in his direction. Several faces turned. Amongst them Paul could see that of big Mrs. Daly, a notorious gossip, agog with curiosity. Blushing, he genuflected hastily towards the altar, and crept down the side of the church into a back pew.

The congregation was quite small, mostly made up of women from the outlying farms who had taken the opportunity of a day's shopping in town to go to Mass. Across the aisle from where Paul sat, Dinny, the local wino, lounged in a pew and snored. He attended all services in order that he might beg at the door of the Presbytery afterwards. Looking around, Paul could see no sign of the little monk.

'He'll have gone out by the main door and be far away by now,' he thought.

He knelt, peering over his clasped hands and waiting his chance to escape. He could tell by the twitching of the flowers on Mrs. Daly's hat that she was still watching him. Whatever would she say to Mum, he wondered? 'Does your Paul have something on his conscience?' Or, 'Could it be he has a Vocation?'

People began to leave their pews, moving into the aisle and trapping him further. Some approached the altar with confidence, their feet tapping smartly along the thin stretch of carpet on the way. Others moved slowly with a show of reverence and awe. Amongst the communicants Paul could see the tall figure of Andrew Bourke, who had grown out of all proportion since leaving school the year before, blushing to the roots of his red hair as he stomped up the aisle in his heavy farmer's boots. Sighing, he sank back. There was nothing he could do but wait for the final blessing to signal his release.

Lulled by the familiar sounds and gestures of the Mass, his mind began to wander. Who was the strange little monk? Where had he come from? How had he managed to disappear so quickly? Why had he stolen the chalice? Somehow, he did not look like an ordinary thief .... He had the most honest eyes I've ever seen, Paul said to himself. Pushing his glasses further up his nose, he abandoned fruitless speculation.

His attention became caught by the flutterings of a butterfly, which having slept the winter in a dark cranny inside the building was roused now by a heady mixture of candlelight and sunshine, and was frantically seeking a way out. Up and down the sunbeams the creature travelled until, exhausted, it came to rest upon one of the stained-glass windows.

Its wings pumped once or twice like a feeble pair of pistons, then closed. The butterfly melted into its background.

Beneath the stained-glass window was a row of wooden saints – quaint copies, by a local craftsman, of ancient stone statues found among the ruins of Kilcarrigan Abbey. The originals, much to Grandfather's annoyance, had been sold for lack of funds, and were now scattered in various museums throughout Europe. 'No substitute for the *real* thing!' he would remark loudly on the infrequent occasions when he came to church. 'A few hands dug deeper into pockets would have done the trick.' He would glower round the members of the congregation, as if accusing each one personally of neglecting his duty to the Past.

As Paul let his eye run along the row of wooden faces (some without noses, others without chins, one or two indeed with only half a face, for the carver had copied the statues in the exact state in which they had been found, mutilated by weather and the hand of man), it fell upon the last statue, shorter, dumpier, and better preserved than the rest. He gasped. 'It's him!' he squeaked.

His words found their way to the flowers on Mrs. Daly's hat. The petals shuddered. 'The boy is as odd as his grandfather,' would be the report, 'talking to himself in church!'

Paul stuffed his fingers in his mouth to prevent himself from saying more. Craning forward, he stared at the statue.

There was no mistaking the resemblance. There was the peaked head like an egg, the plump cheeks, the babyish expression. A knot in the wood even provided the pimple on the chin. 'It *can't* be,' thought Paul, 'unless ....'

The sudden disappearance! The inability of the other boys to see him .... 'But if they couldn't see him why should I? Anyway, ghosts are not like that. They only come at night, and you can see right through them. That fellow was as solid as I am.' And yet .... Shivering with anticipation, he peered at the statue's hands, half-hidden in the shadows. They were empty. Whatever they had been holding had been broken off, and lost. 'Where's the chalice? What have you done with it?' Paul demanded almost angrily between his teeth.

Of course, the statue made no reply. But Paul was about to be given the answer from another source ... Dinny snorted awake. Having cleared his throat raspingly several times and shaken the sleep from his bleary eyes, he cocked his grizzled head, and glared surreptitiously at the statue. Muttering beneath his breath, he began to ease his ungainly form (very ungainly; Dinny always wore several coats, one on top of the other) along the pew. On reaching the end he heaved himself up and peered at something lying on the pew in front. By twisting himself into contortions Paul was able to see what the old tramp was looking at.

It was the monk's parcel!

Paul sat back with a bump. What should he do? He couldn't very well dash across the aisle and snatch the parcel, not with Mrs. Daly's beady eyes upon him. He guessed Dinny was only waiting for the end of the service to lean over and claim what he considered to be a fat prize. This was exactly what happened. No sooner had Father Finnegan intoned 'Amen' than Dinny was on his feet. With surprising dexterity for

19

such a large man in so many coats, he reached out and scooped up the parcel, hiding it under one of his outer garments. Shooting a look of triumph at the statue (almost nodding his thanks, Paul thought indignantly) he made for the door. Without waiting to bow to the altar, Paul was after him.

They reached the street well ahead of the congregation – which was fortunate, for it meant Paul was spared Mrs. Daly's questions and hard looks. Dinny could move very fast when he wanted to; Paul had to run to catch up with him.

'You've no right to that parcel, Dinny,' he panted, falling in line just as the tramp reached the corner and turned into the next road. 'It belongs to a friend of mine.' Dinny grunted. An outcast and solitary by nature, he was unused to people speaking to him and saw no reason to reply. Besides, he considered parcels left lying about his by right. He quickened his pace.

'Dinny!' Paul grabbed the old man's sleeve, digging his feet into the pavement and forcing him to stop. 'Dinny, if you don't give me that parcel I'll call the guard. It isn't yours.'

A gnarled hand, blotched with age and dirt, was dragged from its hiding place, still clutching the parcel. Dinny loomed over him, breathing hard. His coat smelt of damp earth and – wild animals. Foxy! His breath carried traces of cheap sherry. Overwhelmed, Paul began to feel dizzy. Gritting his teeth, he hung on. Through the gathering haze on his glasses he could make out a blob of spittle, rolling sluggishly from the old man's bluish lip to his rusty beard. It clung there like a drop of adhesive someone had squeezed from a tube. Underneath his shaggy eyebrows the tramp's bloodshot eyes looked mean; Paul thought he was going to hit him. He merely

jerked his arm away, and mumbling curses, began to undo the parcel.

What he found was not the bundle of old clothes or food he had expected. It gave him a fright. Uttering a roar like a hurt beast, he shoved the parcel together again and pushing Paul aside, shuffled across the road. Tossing the package into the nearest wastebin he made off, broken boots scuffing the pavement in his haste.

Paul watched the tramp's retreating figure, humped like a tortoise under its many coats. When it had gone he crossed the road and retrieved the parcel. Voices and the slamming of car doors alerted him to the fact that the congregation was leaving the church. In panic he shoved the bulky package beneath his blazer, and took to his heels.

He ran as far as the park, where tall trees and dense shrubs offered seclusion. Choosing a bench away from the main walk, he sat down to examine the parcel. It was wrapped in a piece of rough brown cloth that might have been torn from a monk's habit, and fastened by a leather thong – the strap from his sandal, perhaps? Paul waited until a man with his dog passed by, in an agony of suspense while the animal sniffed around a tree. Then, slipping off the strap, he parted the wrappings of the parcel. Inside, as he knew it would be, lay the chalice.

What should he do with it? Feeling almost as guilty as if he had stolen it himself, Paul drew the cloth back over the chalice, fearful that the sunlight glinting on the silver might attract attention. For a long while he sat staring at the bundle.

He ought to return it to the museum, but he knew by now the building would be closed. Even if it was still open it would be swarming with members of the gardai. There would be questions. How could he answer them? A strange little monk who snatched the chalice from under everybody's noses, then turned himself into a wooden statue. The story was preposterous! He could say he had found the chalice in a wastebin, which was true .... But it sounded unlikely; they would think he had made it up. He would be accused of taking the chalice himself, and be dragged before the court. If only he could get hold of Liam. Alone. He realised with a shock that he did not know where his friend from the museum lived.

He was tempted at that moment simply to throw the chalice into the bushes, and forget it. But he couldn't. Not something so old and precious. Grandfather's most important find! With shaking hands he stuffed the untidy parcel into his schoolbag, and took it home.

By now he really had missed the bus, and had to walk. This made him late, and his mother was cross.

'Where have you been?' she stormed. 'You were due home an hour ago, I was getting worried. Do you not remember you have homework to do? *And* jobs on the farm? You'll have to get your own tea, it's in the oven. I'm giving Tom a bath.'

'I fell in the muck heap.' Tom, Paul's younger brother, smiled angelically. There was little need for him to say so; you could smell him a mile away. At least while they were busy with soap and water, Paul thought, it would give him a chance to hide the chalice. This done to his satisfaction, he helped himself to a dollop of macaroni cheese – turned solid – and sat down to think.

With Tom tucked – well scrubbed – into his bed, his clothes spinning in the washer, Mum was in a better mood when she returned to the kitchen. 'Your grandfather phoned today,' she informed Paul, as she stacked the dishes and took them to the sink. 'He's over at McQuaid's farm, supervising a dig. He was wondering if you would like to join him next week, when you get your holidays? Mr. McQuaid says you can camp in the orchard again, if you bring your tent.'

'Yes, *please*!' Paul's fork dropped with a clatter to his plate. This was just the opportunity he needed! An invitation to McQuaid's farm, tucked in the lea of the mysterious Knocknafeeny Mountains, with the river running by, was always welcome. This year it was doubly so, for it solved his problem. Grandfather would be staying at the farm, so all he had to do was take the chalice to his grandfather. After all he was the one who had found it, so he would know what to do. Paul need not tell him the whole story. Just the bit about Dinny and the wastebin. There was no need to mention the monk.

There was something else that made Paul almost hug himself with the 'rightness' of his plan. The ruins of Kilcarrigan Abbey lay on Mr. McQuaid's land. It was there, Paul supposed, that his grandfather was working. Not only would he be taking the chalice to the man who found it, he would be taking it back to the place where it once belonged!

That night Paul went to bed a happier boy ... but he could not sleep. There were too many unanswered questions. Was the monk *really* a ghost? Had Dinny seen him, too? Why had the monk left his parcel lying on the seat? Was it because the tramp had frightened him? Just what was the connection with the statue? And what was missing from its hands?

Deep in its hiding place under a pile of socks and vests in the top drawer of the chest, the Kilcarrigan Chalice burned through the wood and into Paul's mind.

At last, worn out, he fell asleep.

He was awakened at about two in the morning by the sound of somebody crying.

Chapter 3
Brother Pacifus

'Who's there?'

It was not Tom. When he cried he bellowed, informing the whole world of his grief. This was more a plaintive whimper, like a lost puppy, or .... Paul felt the hair prickling on the back of his neck. A lost soul! He resisted the temptation to pull the bedclothes over his head. Very cautiously, he raised himself on one elbow and peeped down from his top bunk into the room.

He had left the curtains partly open on going to bed. A shaft of moonlight shone through, highlighting the chest of drawers. It fell squarely on the back of a short squat figure in an ill-fitting brown habit with a piece cut out. He seemed to be having trouble wrestling with the top of the chest.

'What on *earth* are you doing?' The spectacle was so ridiculous, Paul forgot that he was frightened. He fumbled for his glasses, putting them on so as to be able to see the ghost more clearly. He did not ask how the little man had got there. He had an uncomfortable feeling he had come through the wall.

'I – can't get it open.' The monk gave up fighting with the chest of drawers. He turned a face lined with puzzlement and grief towards Paul.

'Well, of course not. You don't do it like that.' The monk had spoken in Irish, hard to follow because of an unusual emphasis and accent, but Paul managed to catch most of his words. He was thankful it was one of his better subjects at school and he was able, haltingly, to answer in the same language, 'You don't lift the top. You pull open the drawers. See!'

Careful not to wake his brother in the bunk below, he slipped out of bed and demonstrated. He chose a bottom drawer, avoiding the top one where the chalice lay.

'Ooh!' The monk was apparently impressed. He treated Paul to a beaming, still watery smile, and began to practise this new-found skill, squeaking with delight whenever the drawer slid smoothly into place. Disturbed by the sound, Tom muttered in his sleep. 'Ssh!' Paul warned. 'You'll wake my brother. Then you'll regret it. We can't talk here. Follow me.' He led the way down to the kitchen.

'Do you want something to eat?' he enquired, once the door was safely shut behind them. Whenever he woke at night Paul felt hungry. Ghost or no ghost, this was no exception. He cut himself two thick slices of bread, spreading them with peanut butter to make a sandwich. The ghost looked longingly at the sandwich, but shook his head. 'Fasting,' he explained. 'A *penance*,' he added primly.

'Um ... Pacifus.' Blushing, he introduced himself; he seemed embarrassed by his name. 'Paul Sheean,' replied Paul with his mouth full. Wiping his palm on his pyjama jacket, he half-offered his hand, then withdrew it. It would be awkward, he supposed, if, when their hands met, his should go right through that of the ghost, leaving him clasping nothing. After a moment's hesitation he gave a stiff little bow. Solemnly, Pacifus bowed back.

There followed a long silence, during which Paul munched his sandwich while Pacifus explored the kitchen. He wandered about, touching cooker, deep freeze, fridge, and sink unit with tentative fingers. 'So clean! So shiny!' he kept murmuring. 'What do you do with all them things? Strange, too. How do you light the place?' He had already shown some alarm when the light went on. Now, he stared at the fluorescent bar until he blinked. 'That's not a taper, surely?'

'Of course not,' Paul said. 'It's electricity.' 'Eleck – tree – city?' Pacifus stumbled over the unfamiliar word. 'Never heard of it. Where's the flame?'

'No flame,' said Paul. 'You just flick a switch – You're not getting a demonstration,' he added to himself, 'we'll be here all night.'

He came straight to the point.

'Why do you want the chalice?' he demanded.

The directness of the question upset Pacifus. Withdrawing his eyes from the light fittings, he became tearful again.

'I must take it back,' he sniffed. 'Father Abbot will be angry with me.'

'Why with you?' Paul was curious.

Pacifus looked at him with eyes like two blue goldfish bowls, brimming with tears. 'It – it was I who lost it,' he said flatly.

'Is that why you're doing a penance?'

'No. No!' At this, the ghost became truly agitated, pacing the floor and wringing his hands. In his distress he did not notice a chair pushed away from the table. He slipped right through it, somehow parting in the middle and coming together again on the other side with a sound like a hiccup. 'I shouldn't have done it! I shouldn't have done it!' he wailed.

'Done *what*?' The incident with the chair shocked Paul and made him snappish. He controlled himself with difficulty. 'Look,' he said, 'perhaps you'd better sit down – if you can – and tell me all about it.'

To his relief, Pacifus sat down with no trouble at all (though, being short, his sandals hardly touched the ground). His story came out in spurts, accompanied by sobs and gulps, but eventually Paul was able to fit it all together.

It seemed that in the year 836 (the same date which Mr. O'Mahony had told the boys to remember) Pacifus, a small farmer's son who had been given to the abbey as a sort of 'thank-you' present when he was five, and had grown up with little memory of any other home, was in charge of the care and cleaning of Kilcarrigan Abbey's many possessions. Starting in the kitchen as a potboy, he had worked his way up to be entrusted with the abbey silver. In all this he came under the direct supervision of the Steward, one Brother Gentilis, a tall aristocratic gentleman whom, Paul was soon to learn, Pacifus held in considerable awe ... 'Tis the icy tongue of him,' he confided. 'T would freeze the eyelids off you.'

On the day when the trouble began, Pacifus had been down by the river, giving the silver its weekly wash. Part of his work was rejected ....

'What is *that*?' Brother Gentilis stabbed the side of the chalice with one finger. He kept his nails scrupulously clean, using a small knife for the purpose. They were very long and pointed. Almost as long, Pacifus thought, watching them tapping the crystal rim of the cup, as those of the strange yellow gentlemen from the East he had heard tell about, or – 'God forgive me!' He attempted to suppress the thought, failed, and knew it would cost him thirty 'Hail Marys' for uncharitable musing – perhaps as long as the finger nails of a witch?

'What – is – *that*?' Brother Gentilis was repeating.

'A – a mark, Brother,' Pacifus ventured. 'A small smudge.'

'And what is a "small smudge" doing on a chalice which has only recently been cleaned?' Pacifus cleared his throat nervously. 'Moss, Brother,' he offered.

'Moss?!'

'Yes, Brother. I – I use sphagnum moss for the final polish, it brings it up a treat. Perhaps there was a wee drop of mud amongst the fronds? Or a beetle, maybe?'

'A *beetle*! What do you suppose Father Abbot will say when he finds a beetle smudge on this chalice? The very cup from which he takes wine – the Blood of Christ – during the Mass?' The steward's tones were ominous. 'The beetle must have died,' Pacifus could not help saying sorrowfully.

Brother Gentilis made a sound in his aristocratic nose like the snorting of a very well bred horse. Pacifus was sent back to the river to wash the cup again.

It was, as he explained to Paul, a beautiful day ... 'The sun beating down so hot, I had to make me a hat out of rushes for fear it would frizzle my bald pate. The blackbirds were singing fit to burst their feathered sides, and the fish were just lying there in the shallows fluttering their tails like fans. I propped the chalice against a stone, so the water could lap over it and do its work, and made myself comfortable on the bank. I was waiting for a certain big trout I knew was in the river to make his way upstream. *Not* that I intended to catch him, mind. I would never be so cruel. I just wanted to pick him up in a wee bit of net I keep under my habit, to admire him for a while before putting him back into the water – just to show that I could do it.'

It was getting on for midday. The sun was pouring down hotter than ever. Tilting his makeshift rush hat over his eyes, Pacifus leant back against the soft grass of the bank, and fell asleep ....

'My eyes were only closed for a minute,' he assured Paul. 'When I opened them again, what did I see but the chalice! Bobbing away on the current like a round silver curragh. I was on my feet in an instant, and had broken me a blackthorn staff. The chalice had reached an eddy and was spinning round and round. I had tucked the end of my habit into my girdle, and was about to enter the water ... when I saw him!

'A *huge* fellow, he was. Enormous! He had a coat that shimmered like the ripples of the river. There were wings on his helmet. The sun was dazzling my eyes, so to tell you the truth I thought at first I was meeting an angel ....Until I saw his sword. It was red with blood .... Like me, he was making for the chalice.

'What could I do? I ran after him and fetched him a buffet with my staff. He came at me, then, shouting something in a heathen language and wielding his sword ... Oh, coward that I am!' At this point Pacifus became very tearful, his voice rising to a wail. 'I shouldn't have done it. I should have stood still and been made a martyr.'

'*What* shouldn't you have done?' By now, Paul was totally caught up in the tale.

It took Pacifus some while to get out the words.

'I – I stepped sideways to avoid the blow,' he admitted at last. 'The stones were all covered with weed, and I slipped. The Lochlannach – for I realised, then, that was what he was – came on so fast he tripped over my body and fell into the river. When I got to my feet there he was, lying face down in the water with the blood bubbling out from his throat .... His own sword, you see? It had jerked back and killed him.

'Oh, there's blood on my hands!'

'Rubbish!' said Paul sharply, fearing the little man was about to become hysterical, and would do something unpleasant with the furniture again. 'What did you do then?'

'I panicked,' the ghost replied. 'I forgot all about the chalice, and ran for the abbey.

'I never got there. As I was passing a big rock something hit me on the head and made me see lights .... I *think* I saw angels.' He smiled at the recollection.

The story hung in the familiar air of the kitchen like a dream. To make sure he was awake Paul cut two more thick slices of bread, this time spreading them with marmalade. 'I must take the chalice to Father Abbot,' his companion was saying softly. 'He'll be wondering where it is.'

Paul opened his mouth. And shut it again. It did not seem fair to tell the little fellow that his 'Father Abbot' had died eleven centuries ago – probably slaughtered on that same day when his abbey went up in flames, and Pacifus himself received his death blow.

'I'll be going to the abbey myself, next week,' he said slowly, wondering what Pacifus would say when he found the place was a ruin. 'If you wait you can come with me. We could take the chalice, together.'

Chapter 4
Twentieth Century Vikings!

It is not easy keeping a ghost secret. The rest of that week dragged eternally. Paul, caught up in a whirlpool of events, found himself wishing he had never clapped eyes on the chalice. That his grandfather had never tripped over it. Certainly, he was beginning to regret his promise to help Pacifus.

It seemed the citizens of the town, having neglected to visit their museum for years, were deeply affected by the loss of its famous artifact. Everywhere, people were talking. It felt to Paul, descending from the school bus next morning, conspicuous in his brown blazer, as if all eyes were watching him. One of the 'guilty ones'! School was buzzing like a beehive. Two members of the local gardai had arrived, plus a plainclothes detective. They were in the headmaster's study. Mr. O'Mahony had been in there for 'hours', and had come out looking shaken. All the boys from Paul's class were to be summoned one by one. A bet was on as to whether Francis Tierney was the culprit, or whether it was Fatty O'Rourke. The odds favoured Francis, for Fatty was notoriously slow. When at last Paul's turn came he found himself going hot in the face, and had to take off his glasses and wipe them on the front of his blazer, for he had forgotten his handkerchief.

However, the questions were quite mild and the detective barely glanced in his direction. Trusting they could not read his thoughts, Paul answered as simply and briefly as possible. No, he had *not* taken the chalice from the museum. All he had seen at the time was a hand reaching up. Then it had vanished. As he left the room he overheard Mr. Corcoran the headmaster telling the detective, 'That's Professor Sheean's grandson.' He heaved a deep sigh. Perhaps the relationship gave him an alibi? Nevertheless, he was uncomfortable for the rest of the school day, and was glad when it was time to go home.

At home things were no better. 'Don't *dare* appear while I am out,' Paul had emphasised. He suspected he was the only one capable of seeing the ghost, but was not prepared to take any risks. On returning that evening he had a nasty feeling Pacifus had taken his order too literally, for his bedroom was empty. 'Pacifus,' he hissed, afraid to call too loudly in case someone might hear. 'Pac - i -fus!'

No reply! Suppose he had been fiddling with the chest of drawers, and had got hold of the chalice. Paul rushed to look. But at that moment Pacifus appeared, huddled at one end of the top bunk, looking sulky.

'Where have you been?' he enquired plaintively. 'I've been waiting all day with only my prayers for company. It was like being on a Retreat.'

'I was at school, I told you.'

Pacifus sniffed. 'School! What would the likes of you be doing at a school? Just a farmer's son, like myself. All you need to know is how to tend stock and plant seed, you can learn that at home. Are you aiming for the Church, maybe? Or perhaps it's the Law?'

Paul ignored the note of sarcasm. He did not bother to explain that nowadays everyone went to school, not just the sons of the nobility. There was a strong smell of the farmyard hanging about in his room. He had his suspicions that the ghost had not been there all the time.

'I may have slipped out for a breath of fresh air,' Pacifus admitted when challenged. 'What an odd place your farm is; the byres are almost as clean as your house – and that's saying something. Sure, the High King himself could be entertained in buildings so big and well built. There's a sad lack of anything useful, though. Where are the rakes and sickles for the harvest? Your plough is so large no oxen could pull it. Talking of which, your cattle are deformed. They've not one horn between them. What's that great heap of metal – all wheels and spikes and boxes – in a house of its own?'

'That's our new combine harvester,' Paul told him proudly. 'We don't use rakes and sickles any more. With a combine harvester one man can cut a large three-acre field in under two hours.'

'Black magic!' Pacifus shuddered at the thought. 'One man?' he scoffed. 'What are the rest of them doing, I wonder?'

'Stay – in – this – room,' Paul repeated, 'or I won't take you to the abbey after all.' Even here it was risky.

'What have you got hidden in our bedroom?' Tom demanded, next day.

'Nothing. Why?'

'Only, I thought I saw something move.'

'You're imagining it. Go out and play.'

'Don't want to. It's raining.'

Tom stood stolidly on the top landing, trying to peer round Paul into the bedroom beyond. 'It's my room too, you know,' he reminded his brother. 'If you've got something in there, I've a right to know.'

'No, you haven't. Mind your own business.'

'I think it's an animal.' Tom was triumphant. 'I saw something brown beside the chest of drawers. It looked like a monkey.'

Paul picked up his younger brother by the back of his jersey and manhandled him, protesting loudly, downstairs. He shoved him through the back door and turned the key in the lock. The house reverberated to Tom's bangs and yells, as he kicked at the door panels. Upstairs Pacifus, upset by the noise, wailed like a banshee. Paul braced himself for his mother's questions. But she only said, 'Stop teasing Tom and let him in. It's raining out there, and there's a wind getting up. Don't you hear it?'

It was a relief when the end of the week came at last, and with it the holidays. Paul was able to pack his belongings onto his bicycle, and start along the road to Mr. McQuaid's farm. Only one thing delayed his departure. There was no sign of Pacifus.

'Bother him!' Paul thought sourly. If he waited any longer he would have Tom demanding to come too. 'I'll go on without him,' he decided. 'He can catch up. He seems quite capable of following the chalice.' Sure enough, he had not gone far when the pattering of feet told him he was being followed.

'Wait for me!' Pacifus was all hot and bothered, red in the face, and puffed from running. 'Where have you been?' Paul demanded.

'Nowhere. I – I got lost.' The monk mopped his pink head with his sleeve. It was no use questioning him further. Paul had tried before to find out where the little man went when he vanished. He seemed unable to tell. All he would say was that he felt 'stronger' when he was close to the chalice.

It was only two and a half miles to Mr. McQuaid's farm. Normally, Paul would have done the journey in no time. Today things were different. Thrown off balance by its load, the bicycle wobbled dangerously. Soon he gave up trying to ride. In any case, there was his companion to think of. Tom would have welcomed a lift on the back. Pacifus refused point blank.

'What sort of a cart is that? With only two wheels.' He eyed the bicycle critically. 'Tis only half a cart. What use can that be?' He walked as far from Paul and his bicycle as possible. Presently, hampered by a sandal minus one strap, he started to limp. The road, he complained, was harder than it used to be, it hurt his feet. 'Are you sure we're going the right way?' he grumbled. 'I don't recognise a thing. There should be a big rath on the top of that hill. Why is the pasture divided into those silly little squares with bushes between? Where are the trees?' The road to the abbey, he assured Paul, ran through a forest.

'A dark and terrible place it is, too,' he whispered, 'full of wild beasts. Wild men as well, you'd be likely to be ambushed. Father Abbot only travels with a retinue of the biggest and strongest monks in the abbey. The Lord Fergus goes on the road quite often, of course, but then he has a bodyguard.' Ordinary folk like themselves, Paul learned, did not move about much – only when summoned by the High King to a special assembly, or called to a 'hosting' for a battle, did they take to the roads. In both cases, there would be plenty of them, enough to repel all attackers. The law forbade most people to go beyond the bounds of their lord's land, anyway. Wandering poets and hermits went where they liked, of course. But then, Pacifus said wisely, didn't everyone know they had the power to turn those that annoyed them to stone?

Weren't there big boulders everywhere to show this was true?

'Well, we don't have any of those problems nowadays,' Paul said. 'It's safe to go anywhere.' Pacifus did not agree. The first car to come along had him diving into the ditch.

'What was that?' He crawled out covered with mud, looking shaken.

'Only a car. You must have seen them in town.'

Pacifus denied all knowledge. 'Never saw such a fast chariot in my life,' he declared. 'Where were the horses?'

'There aren't any horses,' Paul said, 'just ....' He stopped, at a loss to know how to explain the workings of a petrol engine to a young man of the ninth century. In any case, the next car had him almost joining the monk in the ditch. It was the squad car, screaming past, blue lights blazing. 'You mustn't look guilty,' he told himself fiercely. 'Whatever you do, don't look round or they'll stop and ask questions. Come on,' he snarled out of the corner of his mouth to his companion, who was pulling up his hood to avoid looking at the traffic. 'If you don't hurry we'll never get to the abbey. Stay close beside me, you're quite safe.'

There came a time when he could have eaten those words – a time when a whole fleet of squad cars might have been welcome.

They had been making good progress. Except for a tractor turning out of a gate (sending Pacifus into hysterics, vowing it to be a machine of Beelzebub, and all the fiends of Hell come for his immortal soul) the road had been empty. They had reached the borders of Mr. McQuaid's land and the farm gate was in sight, when there came a thin metallic whine, like a swarm of angry tin bees, on the road behind them.

'Something's coming!' It was Pacifus, still twitchy from his encounter with the tractor, who heard the noise first. Soon the whine had increased to a roar. It took the form of seven motorcycles, travelling towards them at speed.

'It's Vincent and his "Vikings",' Paul realised. He had not met up with them before, but had often watched them fly past. Vincent and his followers were notorious. A gang of local bullies, they had managed to get hold of secondhand motorbikes, doctoring the engines and 'souping' them up. Calling themselves the 'Viking Raiders', they roared round the countryside, committing petty offences and terrorising those too weak to fight back. If what the other boys at school said was true, they should be avoided at all costs. Wildly, he looked about for cover. The fields were all bare, newly planted with spring wheat. The nearest tree was a good hundred yards away.

'We'll be ambushed!' Pacifus was jumping about in the middle of the road.

'No, we won't. Come here and stay still.' Paul dragged his bicycle almost into the ditch. Bending over, he pretended he was checking a wheel.

The motorcycles came on fast. They shot by, but to Paul's dismay he heard them change gear and come circling back. When he looked, they were lined up in front of him, blocking the road. Their powerful engines spluttered, then died.

Paul felt his heart skip a beat. The riders were faceless, heads encased in bright shiny helmets, like the wing guards of beetles. Behind their smoky visors he could sense eyes, watching him. 'I wonder if they can see ghosts,' he found himself thinking (teeth chattering, Pacifus was muttering prayers for their safety).

It seemed they could not. There was nothing about Vincent's rather vacant expression, as he removed his helmet, allowing his long blonde hair to fall to his shoulders, to show that he had seen anything more unusual than a younger boy bending over his bike. A potential victim!

'What's this?' he mocked. 'A breakdown? Or an accident?'

Chortling at their leader's wit, his followers removed their helmets also, revealing a variety of hairstyles – some spiked and dyed rainbow colours, others shaved to the scalp. Dressed as they were from head to foot in black leather, decorated with studs and clanking with chains, they really did look like the pagan horde they called themselves. 'Lochlannachs!' gasped Pacifus. He crossed himself fervently.

Leaving his bike, Vincent approached. His heavy boots crunched on the tarmac, the white skull and crossbones on his jacket leered from his chest and gave him two faces. Panicked, Paul tried to remount and move on. He was stuck. Following his instructions to 'stay close', Pacifus had straddled the mudguard, and was clutching the wheel.

The Vikings thought his struggles a huge joke. 'Poor little fella can't ride his bike!' giggled one. 'His load is too large, let's lighten it,' suggested another.

'What's your hurry, little Four-eyes?' One of Vincent's big hands – black-gloved – reached out, clumsily snatching Paul's glasses and tossing them into the hedge. Faces blurred as pink blotting-paper hemmed him around, hands like tentacles snatched

at his gear. In no time his bike had been stripped, and all his belongings were scattered about in the road.

'Look what I've found!'

A cry from Pacifus warned Paul that Vincent had come to the saddle-bag, and had discovered the package containing the chalice. 'Not that!' he pleaded, lunging desperately towards his tormentor.

Vincent saw his chance for a game. 'Catch!' he bellowed to one of his gang – a green-haired monster called Shay .... Soon Paul found himself dashing helplessly to and fro, leaping and twisting as the parcel was tossed from one pair of hands to another, always landing just out of his reach .... 'You'll not get it that way,' a small piece of sense whispered inside his brain. He ground to a halt, head spinning, and blinded by tears. 'Please ....' His voice came out as a croak.

Vincent had hold of the parcel. He was growing bored; the game was beginning to pall. 'Let's see what's inside,' he suggested to his expectant companions. His leather fingers started to tear at the wrappings.

The air became loud with suggestions. 'It's the little boy's lunch pack.' 'It's hard. He must have very strong teeth.' 'Watch out, it's a bomb!' 'Nah. It's loot. He's been over to London, and stolen the Crown Jewels.'

'For – the – abbey!'

In his distress, Paul had forgotten about his companion. Just as Vincent's big hands were parting the cloth on the chalice, a small brown bombshell came hurtling through the crowd. 'For the abbey!' It repeated its war-cry. Tonsured head lowered, sandalled feet spurning the ground, it charged ....

delivering the strongest head butt Paul had ever seen, to Vincent's stomach.

The bully reeled, gasping. It was plain from the look on his face he did not know what had hit him. For one second he swayed like a tree. Then he keeled over backwards and fell flat on the road.

His followers gaped at their leader, lying stunned on the ground. They, too, could not guess what had floored him. Fearfully, they eyed one another. As far as they could see there was only one enemy.

Wordlessly, they all turned towards Paul.

CHAPTER 5
THOR'S HAMMER

'What's going on here? Leave the boy alone.'

Rescue had arrived in the shape of Mr. McQuaid driving home from town. He was leaning out of his Range Rover, surveying the scene. 'Leave the boy alone!' he barked.

Faced by a strong-armed farmer, a stout stick laid across the passenger seat, with a collie beside it, lip wrinkled, the Vikings did not wait to explain. Dragging their half-conscious leader between them, they made for their bikes. Vincent was hauled onto his saddle by two burly followers. Booted feet kicked the pedals to action. They sped off as fast as they could the way they had come.

'Are you all right, lad?' Mr. McQuaid got down from his vehicle.

Paul was standing in the midst of his scattered belongings. He seemed in a daze. 'Where is it? Where is it?' he repeated. 'He must have taken it. Where has he gone?'

'Where's what? Did one of those rascals steal something from you?' Mr. McQuaid was concerned.

Paul shook his head. 'Not them,' he said. 'It was ....' He staggered towards the hedge and after some poking and peering found his glasses and put them on. Sight restored, he looked around wildly.

'The monk!' he said urgently. 'He's taken it away. He's gone.'

'There was no monk.' Mr. McQuaid looked at Paul strangely. Had the boy been hit on the head, he was wondering? Gently, he helped him gather up his possessions, and picking up his bike, stacked it into the back of the car. Paul slipped numbly into the passenger seat. Even Bess the collie's glad welcome failed to console him.

'It's all over,' he thought wretchedly, as the car slid the remaining few yards and turned in at the gate. 'There's no ghost. And no chalice. Goodness knows how Pacifus will manage without me to help him. I suppose it's going to be an ordinary holiday after all.'

He could always work beside Gradnfather on the dig, but – Paul leaned his cheek against the silky ruff of the dog's fur, and stared fixedly out of the window. He hoped Mr. McQuaid hadn't noticed the tear leaving his eye to be trapped by the lens of his glasses. Bess's long tongue came out and helped to lick it away. Archaeology was all very well, he reflected. It supplied him with stories to tell them at school – 'I saw the glint of gold in the ground. I snatched up my trowel and scraped away madly. I knew I had found hidden treasure' – Lies, of course. The truth was not nearly so glamorous. Grubbing away in the damp earth, on your hands and knees, for hours ... to be rewarded by a few bits of broken pottery if you were lucky.

No! Paul thought, as he stroked Bess's ears. Grandfather had been right when he said there was no substitute for the real thing. The 'real thing' for Paul at that moment was a ghost – a small man from the Past. 'I'm going to miss him,' he told Bess. 'He was a bit of a nuisance. But I liked him. It's dull, now he's gone.'

The atmosphere of the farm kitchen was anything but dull when Paul entered a few minutes later. Mrs. McQuaid and her pots and pans had been swept aside, and the room was filled with Grandfather and his student helpers. Grandfather was a tall man, anyway. When in a triumphant mood he seemed to grow as you looked at him, sprouting towards the ceiling like a well-cultivated oak. His hair and beard bristled with a life which seemed independent of the man himself. Rather, they seemed charged with electricity coming from the. sunlight which poured through the windows into the large bright room. 'Aah!' was his greeting, 'you're just in time. Come and take a look at this.'

Paul threaded his way through the busy crowd of students coming and going to the scullery with trays of pottery shards, spearheads, harness buckles, for scrubbing and sorting – all the leftover debris of a Viking army, for Grandfather was plotting the route taken by Ulfberht Longarm and his men when they attacked the abbey. 'What an odd looking stone,' he said. 'I never saw one that shape before. Why is it that funny colour?'

'That's not a stone, you omadhaun! Don't they teach you anything at that school of yours? Did you never hear tell of amber?' Professor Sheean had forgotten to remove the eyeglass through which he had been examining the object in his hand. His hazel eye swam disconcertingly towards his grandson, like a jelly-fish. 'This,' he proclaimed, flourishing the translucent yellow 'stone' so that the sunlight, catching it, worked magic, turned it to liquid honey. 'This is a piece of fossilised resin. An ancient drop of sap from a tree which grew long before Man had been invented ....'

Grandfather had the enthusiast's tendency to *go on a bit*. Paul paid little heed to the lecture on the development of amber that followed. 'But ....' he interrupted when at last the old man paused for breath. 'How did the Vikings get hold of it? Why did they want it? It's quite pretty, but what use could it be to a warrior?'

'Use!' Grandfather seemed to find the word offensive. He let the eyeglass drop from his eye, catching it deftly and stowing it away with the many other bits and pieces in his pocket. 'They had a use for it all right. There was a big trade in amber. The Vikings were vain fellows. Very fond of jewelry and the like. They were also deeply superstitious, and they believed that amber had magic properties. After all doesn't every schoolboy know that when you rub it, amber has magnetic power. This piece, now, has been carved into a charm. What shape would you say it was, exactly?'

Paul accepted the piece of amber from his grandfather. It felt surprisingly light and smooth, and strangely warm, as if fired by the bead of sunlight glinting at its heart. He held it up to his eye and looked through it, seeing the room change to gold. Taking it away again, he examined it more carefully. 'It looks like a small axe,' he said, 'only it has two blades, one on either side of the haft.'

'Not an axe. The blades are blunt, don't you see?' Grandfather's beard quivered with excitement as he bent over the amber. 'The piece has been carved to represent a hammer,' he explained. 'No ordinary hammer, either. The hammer of a God! Thor the Thunderer, God of War. After his father Odin, he was the greatest of all the Vikings' gods. When thunder rolled men said it was Thor, driving his chariot across

47

the skies. This was his weapon. "Mjollnir the Destroyer". It never missed, and no one could stand against it. What better charm could a Viking warrior have when going into battle?'

'So he would have worn this round his neck?'

'Usually. But I'm thinking, from its size and from the fact that there is no sign of its being pierced – no link for a chain – that this talisman comes from the pommel of a sword. It would be a richly ornamented weapon with jewels in its hilt, for amber was expensive. Only the very highest in the land could afford a piece as big as this. The sword I'm thinking of would have been the property of a prince.'

'That means you think ...?'

Grandfather shut his mouth like a trap. His beard jutted fiercely. 'I'm only guessing, mind,' he warned, 'and don't tell my students I make guesses. Such speculation is not allowed. An archaeologist is like a detective. He builds up his picture from the evidence only, using the facts as he finds them.'

A scene flashed before Paul's eyes. He saw a small man in a ridiculous rush hat standing in the shallows of a river. Shabby brown habit tucked above his knees, he watched appalled as a beautiful silver chalice was carried rapidly beyond his reach. Around his ankles the water of the river was running red, stained with the blood of a Viking warrior. A prince? Surely only Ulfberht Longarm would have worn the winged helmet and splendid coat of mail of Pacifus's description? What was it Mr. O'Mahony had said? – 'There is no record of Ulfberht ever reaching home' – Was that because a frightened little monk had stepped sideways to avoid a blow? The sword jutting from the swaying body's throat – Paul screwed up his eyes to concentrate upon the scene – was there an amber charm in its hilt? ... 'Where did you find ...?' he began to ask. But Grandfather, the enthusiasm of the moment past, had replaced his eyeglass with his gold-rimmed spectacles, and was regarding his grandson severely over the top.

'The gardai have informed me the Kilcarrigan Chalice has gone missing,' he observed, 'and that your school was somehow instrumental in its loss.'

'That's not true. It's wasn't our fault,' Paul wanted to shout indignantly. But he thought better of it. What could he say, anyway? Now Pacifus had removed the chalice, robbing him of the opportunity to hand it over. Discreetly, he chose that moment to retreat to the orchard to pitch his tent.

When he came back again the kitchen was greatly changed.

Mrs. McQuaid had won back her domain. All signs of archaeology had been tidied away, and the great scrubbed wood table was spread with a delicious supper.

It was a jolly meal, for the students were great talkers and jokers. One young man who ate faster than the rest left the table, and fetching his guitar, sat in the corner strumming soft tunes. At the top of the table Grandfather, annoyance over the loss of the chalice and triumph at the finding of the amber both put aside in favour of good food, beamed upon everybody like a long benevolent Santa Claus. Mrs. McQuaid, beaming almost as broadly, piled their plates high with succulent slices of boiled bacon, mounds of colcannon, and great pools of parsley sauce, until Paul felt he was about to burst. Declining a second helping of apple pie and cream, he excused himself and went out into the yard to digest his meal.

The moon had risen, soaking everywhere with a silver wash so that the roofs of the sheds and barns looked wet with it. Behind him in the kitchen Paul could still hear the throbbing notes of the guitar, while from a nearby hen-house came the placid 'tut-tutting' of the hens, telling each other of their dreams. In the cowshed, a cow lowed sleepily. Bess, her white legs and chest bleached by the moonlight, went trotting across the yard. Paul called to her, but she had work to do helping Mr. McQuaid to check the sheep, and dutifully ignored him.

At the far end of the yard, light from a storeroom window was spilling onto the stones to form a golden rectangle in an otherwise silver world. Close to this first rectangle a second, narrower shaft of gold indicated that someone had left the door slightly open. 'I had better shut it,' Paul thought, knowing from past visits that this was where the finds from the dig were categorised and stored. Grandfather would be cross if he knew the door had not been closed.

Once outside, he was tempted to go in. There was no one there; the room was empty, lit by a naked lightbulb dangling from the ceiling. Long trestle tables had been set in rows, and on them artifacts from the Past were lined in neat formation, like oddly shaped soldiers in a model army. It was not difficult to spot the piece of amber amongst the humbler ranks of earthenware and iron. Reaching over, Paul touched the double-headed hammer with deferential fingers. Was he mistaken? Or did the charm feel hotter than before? He picked it up ....

A weird tingling sensation running up his arm almost caused him to drop it and cry out .... In a dark corner, someone laughed.

Paul whipped round. He had only a brief glimpse of glittering eyes beneath the helmet, and the glimmer of a coat of mail in the gloom. Bolting for the door, he slammed it behind him as he ran for the safety of the moonlit yard.

CHAPTER 6
RAIDERS OF A PAST DAWN

Paul ran and ran. He ran until he felt his chest would burst and he would have no breath left for running. Finding himself in the orchard, he caught hold of the slim trunk of a tree and clung there, trying to still his beating heart so that he could listen for the sound of following footsteps. He heard nothing – only the uneasy shifting of a bird in the branches above his head. Under the light of the full moon the trees stood out like well-executed charcoal drawings. Nothing moved. He took a deep breath and let it out again. Had he lost one ghost only to find another? However faint, this one was far more frightening! At least Pacifus had been friendly. It was when he dug for his handkerchief to mop his face and clear his glasses that he discoveredthat in his panic he had brought 'Thor's Hammer' with him.

Paul looked at the amber charm in dismay. He had done it again! Landed himself with something that didn't belong to him. 'Most likely I'm landed with its terrible owner, too,' he thought, shuddering at the memory of the cruel face in the storeroom.

'*This* is going back,' he decided, 'as soon as it is light tomorrow morning.' He was relieved to find, when he drew his fingers over it, that the little hammer felt quite cool. No unpleasant vibrations ran up his arm; 'Mjollnir the Destroyer' seemed harmless for the present. Just to make sure, he put it well below his pile of clothes when going to bed, leaving the pile as close to the tent door as possible.

Sleep evaded him. Whenever his eye travelled to the door of the tent he imagined a ghostly hand stealing under the flap, searching for the charm. Rigid with fear, he lay stiff as a post in his sleeping bag, a brief doze only bringing wild dreams of bloody battles and leaping flames. Pacifus fled down an endless avenue of boulders (perhaps 'wild men' turned to stone by the hermits and poets he had mentioned?) Behind each boulder lurked a Viking, battleaxe ready to smash his poor shaved head .... When at last the first rooster crowed in the farmyard, Paul got up and dressed by the beam of his torch.

'I must find Pacifus and warn him,' he thought, the dream still raw in his mind. Whatever happened, the ghosts must not meet, or the result might spell disaster. By now, Pacifus could have reached the Abbey. Paul pictured the little monk standing lost and bewildered amidst the ruins. No Father Abbot. No Brother Gentilis, even!

'On the other hand, he may not have got there yet,' he comforted himself. 'With everything so changed it may be taking him some time. Perhaps I can waylay him.' He considered for a moment whether to leave the charm, or take it with him. In the end, he decided on the latter course. At least he would know where it was, and as soon as the storeroom was unlocked after breakfast he would put it back. Somewhat reluctantly, he slipped it into his pocket.

The dawn chorus was in full voice by the time he emerged from his tent. Blackbirds were laying fresh claim to their territories, robins challenging each other in the thickets. Somewhere a woodpigeon cooed persistently. From the fields beyond the orchard came the cracked voices of the sheep calling to their young, the lambs answering in flat childish trebles. As yet, there was little light beneath the trees and a soft mist clung to the branches, hanging down like strands of wool. When he came out into the open the sun was beginning to rise above the Knocknafeeny Mountains. Enthralled, he stood for a while to watch the moving display of the dawn, then recalling his mission, turned and made for the boreen leading to the fields where the abbey ruins lay.

It was dark in the boreen, for the sun was not yet high enough to penetrate the thick hawthorn hedges on either side. They grew tall, curving to form a tunnel over the path. Unable to see clearly where he was going, Paul kept falling into ruts, splashing into puddles which remained after the rain of a few days before. He had gone about halfway, when he became conscious of a sharp burning sensation coming from the pocket where he had the charm.

Oh no! Despite the unevenness underfoot, Paul quickened his pace. For all his effort, the burning grew worse, searing through the thin fabric lining of his pocket and hurting his leg. The charm seemed to be heavy as well as hot, holding him back. He longed to be rid of it, but the idea of plucking it out with his bare hand to throw it away was more than he could face. Gritting his teeth, and keeping his eyes fixed on the 'O' of daylight at the end of the tunnel, somehow he kept going. Convinced that he could hear footfalls on the other side of the hedge, he broke into a run, bursting out, blinded by sudden sunlight, through an open gate and travelling several yards across the field before sliding to a halt .... He stood up to his ankles in the dew-soaked grass, and gasped.

The footfalls (real or imaginary) had ceased. The burning sensation was gone, leaving his leg merely feeling numb. He was, he knew from last night's conversation at the supper table, at the edge of the field where the dig was taking place. On a small hillock, two fields away, a clump of sycamore shielded the abbey ruins, a gang of rooks quarrelling in a disorderly manner above their untidy nests in the topmost branches. The excavation itself was at the foot of a shallow dip – the remains of an old quarry – near the centre of the field. Some brightly coloured buckets and a roll of plastic sheeting had been left under a furze clump in readiness for the day's work. Paul saw the buckets in a quick flash, like a film slide on a screen before the click of the projector sends it on into the dark. He saw the clump of furze, the sycamores, the squabbling rooks in the same way .... Then the scene was changed.

The buckets and the plastic sheet had disappeared. In their place stood a rickety handcart loaded with sand. Two shovels had been thrust into the top of the heap. There was no sign of the furze bushes; a loosely woven wattle fence cut off the quarry. Whereas a moment before Paul's ears had been assailed by the clamour of the rooks, now there was an eerie silence, broken only by the distant bell-like warning of a blackbird. Through the haze veiling the newly risen sun, he could see that the sycamores had been replaced by an orchard of apple trees, clothing the slope and jutting into the fields, which – all hedges gone – had become one large meadow, with flowers speckling the long grass. Beyond the meadow and the orchard he caught sight of high stone walls.

Paul blinked. Nervously, he ran his fingers through his hair, making it stand up even more than usual. He pushed his glasses further up his nose and looked again, just to make sure he was seeing right. 'Ghosts are one thing,' he said to himself. 'They can be good like Pacifus, or they can be bad like Ulfberht Longarm, but at least between hauntings they leave you alone in familiar surroundings. This is different!' He had heard stories of people who had stepped by chance into the World of Faerie, finding everything subtly changed. In all the stories those people had to remain where they were for a hundred years. 'I'm going back,' thought Paul, 'before it's too late.'

He turned to find the gate had vanished. There was no boreen. An impenetrable forest blocked his path.

'There'll be wild beasts in that forest.' Paul recalled what Pacifus had said. 'Wild men, too.' He had little doubt that he had stepped – or more probably, thinking of the burning sensation and the following footsteps, he had been driven – back in Time. To the year 836, the time of Ulfberht Longarm, Brother Gentilis, Father Abbot, and Pacifus himself. Those stone walls emerging from the mist above the apple trees, strong and complete, well-chiselled stone fitting snugly upon well-chiselled stone – rare in an era when most buildings were made of wattle and thatch, and a credit to the mason monks who had raised it to the glory of God – could only belong to Kilcarrigan Abbey. As if to confirm that the building was occupied, at that moment a bell rang out behind the walls, summoning the brothers to Prime, the first office of the day.

There was nothing to be done, Paul decided, but to walk up to the abbey and entrust himself to the hospitality of the monks. At least he was known to one of them! He was about to put this plan into action when there came a rustling in the trees behind him, and a beautiful stag stepped out of the forest onto the meadow grass.

Paul held his breath. He had never been near so large and wild an animal before. The creature was truly superb. Its winter coat had only recently been shed, so that its flanks gleamed reddish gold, matching the colour of the rising sun. Its velvety antlers were just beginning to sprout the promise of a magnificent autumn crown. Treading the meadow like a prince, it lowered its head, and as if bestowing a favour on the grass began to graze. Its ears moved restlessly while it cropped, but it seemed unaware of the boy and came so close he might have touched it. He had begun tentatively to put out his hand when something disturbed the creature's meal. With a grunt of alarm its head shot up. White showed at the corners of its eyes. Its nostrils flared, nervously testing the air in the direction of the quarry. Wheeling about, it bounded silently back into the forest. Paul remained tense. A gentle dawn breeze had brought him the sound which had startled the stag. It was the sound of human voices.

Paul abandoned his decision to go to the abbey. Creeping towards the wattle fence, he crouched low, and parting the loosely woven mesh, peered through.

The quarry was deeper than he had expected, and newly worked. Marks of picks and shovels scarred its sides. A group of men were seated down below. They were very still, and Paul judged they had been waiting all night, for the dew was clinging to the woollen fibres of their cloaks, muting the bright colours. Tiny drops formed a mist over their helmets and on the wooden shields, decorated with great bronze discs, which lay at each man's side. Now and then a warrior shifted slightly to ease his cramped limbs, or fingered his axe or short sword as if to reassure himself that it was there. They were well-armed, so what were they waiting for, Paul wondered? The dawn? It had passed. A signal, perhaps? Or the report of spies? Were they waiting for their leader? Anxiously, he scanned the faces of the warriors. Fierce weatherbeaten faces, for the most part bearded. Those who were clean-shaven were merely boys. The face he had glimpsed in the storeroom was not there. Among the dew-sprinkled helmets there was not one of the winged magnificence described by Pacifus.

Paul let the wattle slip back into place. Easing himself to the lea of the cart, he hid beneath it. His thoughts were racing. Was it possible, to alter the course of history? What would happen if he made a dash for the abbey to warn the monks that the Vikings had arrived?

Even as the idea took shape he felt the ground nearby vibrate, and knew he was too late. Ulfberht Longarm was standing only a few yards off. His back was turned. His helmeted head was lowered. He was searching for something.

It took all Paul's will-power not to cry out loud. It did not need the object in his pocket, recharged with heat and burning like a brand into his flesh, to tell him what the Viking chief was looking for. So this was the cause of the delay. This was why, on that fateful day in the ninth century, the monks had been left to go about their peaceful duties all the morning (duties which presumably had not taken them to the quarry). Ulfberht Longarm had mislaid his lucky charm! Deeply superstitious, he had been reluctant to storm the abbey without the power it gave. Even later, when despite his better judgement the battle had begun, he had not abandoned his search. Obsessed by it, he had returned to the river where he and his men had landed. There, his eye had been caught by a glint of silver on the water. He had disturbed the slumbers of a little monk ... and had met his doom! Fascinated, Paul's eyes travelled to the jewelled hilt at Ulfberht's belt. Above the rich cluster of rock crystals, carnelians, and garnets was an empty gap. Time and again as he searched, the Viking's hand returned to the pommel of his sword, his thumb running nervously over the vacant socket which had held the amber charm – an amber charm which, at that moment, was burning a hole in Paul's pocket! 'You're never going to find it,' he breathed, 'even if you search for more than a thousand years.'

His words were defiant, but he was in need of all the reassurance his superior knowledge could give, for his leg was in agony. The amber seemed to be dragging at his pocket, threatening to pull him out from underneath the cart. Clutching one of its wooden wheels, he watched Ulfberht Longarm drawing nearer. The toe of the Viking's boot was almost upon him ... when there came a second tolling of the abbey bell.

Ulfberht halted. His trousered leg, criss-crossed with leather gartering (all that Paul could see from where he was crouching), tensed. From down below, in the quarry, came a faint clink of metal as the warriors unsheathed their swords. Paul guessed the reason for their readiness. Prayers over, the monks were being summoned to their daily work. Soon the abbey gates would be opened, and those whose duty it was to work upon the land would be descending to the meadow. Already, the lowing of cattle informed him that the herdsmen were about to drive their beasts down to the rich grass. Ulfberht was starting to retreat towards the quarry. Paul came to a rapid decision. If he could do nothing else, he would try to keep Ulfberht Longarm in the open long enough for the herdsmen to see him and raise the alarm. 'Wait, Ulfberht Longarm,' he called. 'I have something for you.' Biting his lip against the pain, he took 'Thor's Hammer' from his pocket, and crawled out from underneath the cart.

Slowly, Ulfberht turned towards him. Paul had a clear view of blue eyes hard as sapphires beneath the helmet, a jagged white battle scar running across the man's bronze cheek to his drooping blonde moustache. The scar puckered his face, tilting his mouth into a sardonic grin. Despite his permanent false smile the Viking seemed uneasy. His eyes shifted here and there. He gripped his sword.

'I don't believe he can see me. I am a ghost in his time, just as he is a ghost in mine.' The realisation came as a shock, but Paul decided to use it. Invisible or not, he sensed the Viking knew that he was there. 'Come on, Ulfberht Longarm,' he coaxed. 'Follow me.' Holding the charm out towards the man, not daring to take his eyes off him, he began to walk backwards across the grass.

Over the meadow herbs, they went; Paul, blinded by tears of pain, stumbling slightly, Ulfberht following with measured steps as if drawn against his will upon a cord. The sun, clear of the mist and higher now (beginning to gain a heat that would force a small monk, later in the day, to weave a rush hat against its rays, then fall into a doze), drew fire from the wings of the Viking's helmet. It danced in myriad reflections on the bronze discs of his mail. It ran in liquid flame along his sword, causing the dragons engraved there

to twist and writhe. 'He's shining like a beacon. The herdsmen can't miss him.' Despite the agony in his hand Paul laughed aloud. Behind him he could hear the trampling of hooves coming through the orchard, the beasts' bellowing calls, the shouts of the men who drove them.

His moment of triumph was short-lived. Just as the first horned head emerged beneath the branches, his foot caught on a large ant heap, his ankle twisted, and he was flung sideways. As he reached out to save himself, the amber flew from his hand, catching the light as it arched towards the ground.

Ulfberht saw it! In three strides he had reached the spot where it had fallen.

'He mustn't have it!' Wriggling snakelike, Paul managed to get to the charm just as Ulfberht's foot, clad in soft leather, came down beside it. Curling his fingers round the piece of amber, he struggled to his knees. He flung it with all his strength towards the orchard, and the approaching herdsmen. As it hit the earth there came a flash of lightning, followed by a deep low rumble ....

'Thor! God of War! He's angry. He's after me!' Burying his head in his arms, Paul threw himself full length upon the ground.

The lightning ceased. Gradually, the thunder rolled away, leaving a faint echo in the Knocknafeeny Mountains. Was it thunder? Or the cawing of the rooks above the sycamores? Paul dared to look up.

Ulfberht Longarm was no longer there. The dense forest, the sprawling orchard, and the flowery meadow had melted away. Bewildered, he looked about, half expecting the herdsmen to have reached the pasture, their long-horned charges spreading out to enjoy the lush sweet grass. The familiar pattern of fields was back in place. Over by the disused quarry, the archaeologists' bright buckets gave a reassuring splash of colour against the dark background of the furze. To make doubly sure Paul ran to the gate, and looked along the boreen leading to the farm. All was well! He crept to the edge of the quarry and peeped over, just to check there were no Viking warriors left behind.

Everything was in order. There was the neat working of the dig, the turf rolled back to expose the bare clay criss-crossed by lines of white tape to form a grid. Numbered markers jutting from the soil kept a record of each find. As always, Grandfather had been particular about every detail of the excavation. It was unlike him to leave a bundle of old sacks right in the middle of the work. 'Still, I suppose he knows what he's doing,' Paul thought. He did not dwell upon the subject, for his head was throbbing after his strange experience. Also, his trip into the Past had made him hungry! With his mind on one of Mrs McQuaid's delicious fried breakfasts, he was about to turn away ... when the bundle of old sacks groaned.

Pacifus! In an instant, Paul had slithered to the bottom of the dip. Ignoring all the rules, he ran straight across the archaeologists' neat work, jumping the tapes as he went. As he knelt beside it, the bundle stirred. A face, white with shock, disentangled itself from the mass of brown material. Two round blue eyes swimming with tears looked up into his. Pacifus was bound hand and foot, trussed up like a chicken.

'Whatever happened? How did you get here?' Paul looked in vain for a piece of broken glass – or a sharp stone – something to cut the bonds. In the end, the cords – woven rushes fortified by some sort of gut – just fell away when he touched them, and crumbled to dust ('I suppose they would,' he thought, 'if they were eleven hundred years old').

'The Lochlannachs. They caught me. I was almost at the abbey when they crept up behind. It was your fault. If only you wouldn't go interfering with other people's possessions!'

'What do you mean?' Paul's mind flew to 'Thor's Hammer', it's extraordinary power, able it would seem to take him to and fro across the centuries. 'I wasn't even there when .... I was ...' He broke off. It was pointless to argue, it only made his head throb worse. Pacifus, he noticed with unease, was rubbing his numbed wrists and ankles with his hands. Hands which were definitely – and disastrously – empty! 'Where's the chalice?' he demanded. 'You didn't give it to them, did you?'

'Of course not.' Two pink spots of indignation appeared on Pacifus's pale cheeks. 'When I heard them coming I hid it in a wee small wood.'

The 'wee small wood' turned out to be a hedge (not a familiar mark on the ninth century landscape, so Pacifus could be forgiven for his mistake). Search as they might, from one end to the other, the pair were unable to find the chalice anywhere.

'Are you *sure* this is the right place?' Paul's hair was standing up like the bristles on the yard brush; dead leaves and twigs decorated his clothes.

'Positive.' The ghost was looking remarkably tidy, but of course he had been conducting his search from the *outside* of the hedge, 'while,' Paul thought bitterly, 'giving instructions to the person *inside* .... It's not here,' he said sulkily.

'It must be. I can remember that broken bit of a tree over there. I .... Oh, St. Mullarkey! What's that?!' At the sound of footsteps on a nearby path, Pacifus disappeared. All that was left was the pink top of his head above the fallen tree he had been indicating. Briefly, the rest of his face followed his tonsure. 'Hide! Quick!' he hissed. 'The Lochlannachs are coming back. They'll get you.'

'That's not a Lochlannach, you idiot.' Paul found himself dissolving into giggles. 'It's a pig!'

Clearly, there could be no mistaking it for anything else. The pig was a superb example of its kind: large in every way, as broad as it was long. Its delicate cloven hoofs picked their way over the rough stones of the path, as if they were supporting nothing heavier than a pink balloon – a pink balloon, with two ears shaped like shovels, a pair of roguish piggy eyes, and an inquisitive tip-tilted nose. The ears were black, and expressively mobile. There was a black ring, rather like a pirate's patch, round one of its eyes. Its back was decorated here and there with spots like ink drops, and there was one particularly large splodge, as if somebody had aimed the ink bottle at its tail. If you looked closely, you were struck by the fact that above its many chins the animal wore an idyllically happy grin.

The pig was closely followed by his owner. He was large in every way, too, and also wore a happy smile upon his face.

'Why, it's Michael All-alone! With Tantony.' The pig might have grown somewhat since Paul had seen him last, but he recognised the big man immediately. Michael was a close neighbour of the McQuaids'. As his name implied, he lived alone, preferring the company of his donkey, his pig, and his ducks and hens to that of people. Somehow, as a child and on his own, Paul had managed to penetrate this magic circle, and over the years the two had become great friends.

Michael halted, his bright smile fading. 'It's only me,' Paul assured him. The big man was staring straight past him at the fallen tree. His eyes – black, like those of his pig – became round as berries. Presently, however, his smile broke out again, growing broader and broader until it threatened to split his face in two. 'Come out of that,' he called softly. 'Don't be hiding yourself away. Come out and let me look at you.'

'You can see him!' Paul did not know whether to be jealous or not. Fond as he was of Michael, he was not sure he wanted to share his new companion, having only just found him again. Blushing, Pacifus emerged slowly from behind the tree. He stood modestly looking at his sandals while the big man walked round him, examining him from every angle.

'Why wouldn't I see him?' he demanded. 'Isn't he as plain as the dots on Tantony's back? And a good deal more real than most people I know. You're very welcome,' he told Pacifus. 'I'm honoured to have this visitation. I could do with a friendly ghost, it will make a change from those other divils the arkimelogical men have let loose about the place. Stomping around outside my house all night! Waving their axes. Threatening to set the place alight, and roast me and my pig together. Sure, they're not civilised at all!'

'The Vikings! You've seen the Vikings?' This was almost too much. That Michael – a grown-up, however different – might see one ghost was acceptable; that he seemed to be deep in the same adventure was, to say the least, bewildering. Paul gaped at him.

'Indeed I have.' Michael turned accusingly on Paul. 'Tis all your grandfather's fault,' he stated. 'Scratching about in the clay, the way he does. "Dig up the Past, and you dig up trouble," me Gran always says. Isn't the Past always there, anyway? Like dust in the corners, she tells me. What's the point of stirring it with a broom, so it comes up and chokes you?'

Michael's Gran? So she was mixed up in this! The old lady had – certain Powers. Paul's mind began to work fast. If he had to share his adventure with anyone, what better person than Michael All-alone? He could be useful. 'Look,' he said aloud, 'would you do me a favour? Look after this fellow for a while.' He indicated Pacifus, who was staring suspiciously at Tantony. 'I can't take him back to the farm, with all those students about. Also,' he lowered his voice, 'I have things to do.'

Michael was charmed by the idea. Pacifus was not. It was necessary to find the chalice at once, he insisted; Father Abbot would be waiting. Besides, having summed up Tantony's size, and considerable weight, he was not too happy to be going with him.

'Does that pig bite?' he enquired, preparing to back away behind the tree (Tantony, growing bored, was beginning to take too great an interest in his toes). 'Brother Agricula, our swineherd, says they can be very fierce at times.' It took a deal of persuasion – plus indignant assurances on Michael's part that his pig was 'very kind' – to get him going. Paul watched with relief as the three oddly assorted figures moved away along the path, Tantony leading at an enthusiastic bounce, Michael striding on his long legs, and Pacifus – habit raised delicately above his ankles – trotting to catch up. When they disappeared, he turned back to his search.

The chalice could wait, he decided. After all, everyone knew it was missing. So there was no rush. He could take his time – and choose his moment – to 'discover' it, and become a hero! What was far more worrying was the fact that he had thrown away the amber. He glanced at his watch. Luckily, it was unaffected by its 'time trip'. It said five to eight. By now they would be sitting down to breakfast. It was only a case of how many slices of toast, thickly spread with Mrs. McQuaid's homemade marmalade, Grandfather would eat, before producing his keys and strolling across the yard to the storeroom. He would have to hurry! It was not going to be easy to find where something – thrown away in the ninth century – had landed in the twentieth. He set off at a run.

As he drew nearer to the boreen he slowed. To go along it would be to relive a nightmare. Suppose Ulfberht Longarm had returned and was waiting for him at the other end? What if he should find himself once more in the Past? ... It was almost with relief, therefore, that he realised the sound he had been listening to for some while – but had been ignoring because of other worries – was the harsh, unmistakably twentieth century noise of motorcycle engines. Vincent and his 'Vikings'. They were at the dig! Slithering through the mud and splashing through the puddles, Paul dashed towards the gate.

It so happened that Vincent and his followers had been to an all-night 'rave'. They were indulging in a final celebration before going home to bed. The scene which met Paul's eyes, as he arrived puffing and panting in the field, bore all the marks of a motorcycle scramble.

Buckets, tape, and plastic – the archaeologists' paraphernalia – were scattered to the winds. Everywhere, the ground was scarred by tyres. Mud flew as, with blood-curdling yells, the Vikings drove their bikes at the lip of the dig, down one side, and up the other.

'Stop! Please, stop.' Protest was much too late. And useless. In any case, his feeble cries were drowned out.

Gathering in formation, the Vikings hurtled towards him. He had scarcely time to leap aside as the engines screeched past, to be swallowed, along with a final tidal wave of mud, by the dark mouth of the boreen.

Paul staggered to his feet. For one moment he was uncertain whether he was in the 'Here and Now', or 'There' and 'In the Past'. He shook his head to clear it and in so doing dislodged a splat of mud which had landed on his glasses. What was it that had caught his eye as Vincent had screamed by and almost knocked him flying?

As realisation dawned, he flung back his head and laughed aloud. Spreading his arms, he did a comic dance of triumph on the rutted ground. A new emblem had appeared on Vincent's bike, fixed to its handlebars. A knob of amber! Paul had noticed the flash of sunlight at its heart as the bully sped past him. Thor's Hammer!

'Oh, Vincent!' he crowed. 'Just you wait till you meet its owner. One Viking faced by another. That's going to be interesting!'

Chapter 8
Chaos In Both Directions

By the time he reached the end of the boreen, elation melting, Paul was in a more sombre mood. So far, he realised, he had achieved nothing. Two important archaeological finds were still missing. He heard his grandfather's roars of rage long before he came to the farmyard.

Professor Sheean was standing at the open storehouse door. His gold-rimmed spectacles were askew. He was tearing his hair in fury and disbelief. 'Who could have done this?' he demanded. Paul, inching his way through the gathering crowd of students, had a clear view of the interior of the storeroom, and felt himself go cold and sick with dread. So *this* was what Ulfberht Longarm could do when he was angry!

No human hand could have caused such chaos. The light bulb had been torn from its moorings, taking half the ceiling with it. There appeared to have been some sort of minor explosion on the floor, for in one corner a small crater yawned. Everywhere, the walls were deeply gashed as if attacked by someone with an axe. What remained of the trestle tables was fit only for matchsticks, while their neatly arranged contents were reduced to a heap of powdered clay and twisted metal on the ground. Shakily, Professor Sheean took a few steps into the room. Down on his hands and knees, he rummaged amongst all that was left of his carefully excavated pieces from the Past. At last he raised a head whitened and smeared by dust. 'The amber is gone.' He spoke hoarsely. 'It isn't here. Someone has stolen it.'

Paul could have crept away unnoticed. He could have stood his ground and given an explanation of events. Instead, he chose to reshape the truth.

'They were at the dig, too,' he said, his voice almost as hoarse as his grandfather's in the disbelieving silence. 'I saw them.'

'Saw whom? What are you talking about, boy?' Professor Sheean was on his feet.

Paul swallowed hard. He met his grandfather's hazel glare unflinching. 'Vincent, and his Vikings,' he said clearly. 'They were riding up and down across the dig. They have the amber. I saw it on Vincent's handlebars.'

'What!?' The word could have hit the Knocknafeeney Mountains and bounced back again. Beard bristling, Grandfather was definitely back in charge. 'Terence!' he bellowed at one of the students. 'Off to the house with you. Dial 999, and get the guards. Everyone else! Grab your tools, and come with me.' Paul found himself pushed hurriedly aside. He was almost trampled down by the army of students marching towards the dig.

Time for breakfast at last, he decided. But not before he had washed off the worst of the mud at the scullery sink. Somewhat cleaner and with hair plastered down as best he could, he presented himself to Mrs. McQuaid in the kitchen.

The meal was over, but that did not prevent Mrs. McQuaid frying eggs, bacon, black pudding, tomatoes and sausages, and insisting he should follow it with piles of toast and marmalade and several cups of hot sweet tea. He was just coming to the end of this marathon feast when he heard his grandfather come back into the house, going to the telephone. 'Better make myself scarce,' he decided. 'I don't want any more questions.' Thanking Mrs. McQuaid for her kindness, and assuring her he really couldn't eat another thing, he wiped his mouth and left the table.

Some of the students were gathered round the storeroom door, talking excitedly, and reminding each other that nothing must be touched until the gardai had been. Paul skirted the group. Bess, lying in a sun patch beneath the wall, rose to her feet and followed him. 'I wish collies had a better sense of smell,' Paul said to her. 'You might be useful searching out the chalice. I don't suppose silver smells much, though.' Dog at his heels, he was just approaching the hedge and the fallen tree when an extraordinary cacophony of noises coming from the direction of Michael's cottage made him turn tail and fly that way. Squawks! Squeals! Yells! And over it all the hysterical, two-toned braying of a donkey. Bess added to the din. Barking madly, she shot ahead. Wishing he hadn't eaten so much breakfast, Paul followed. He burst through the shelter belt of trees to find himself faced, for the second time that morning, with devastation.

Michael's smallholding – a yard with a duck pond in the middle, one or two tiny fields, and a cluster of corrugated iron sheds leaning against the whitewashed cottage – was normally a model of neatness. Usually, the yard was swept so that you could have eaten your dinner off its stones (you could have taken a bath in the duckpond!). The tiny garden behind its well-clipped box hedge was laid out in squares of onions, potatoes, and cabbages that were the envy of the district (and not a weed in sight). Geraniums in clean scrubbed pots brightened the windowsills of the little house, and the metal milk churn beside the blue front door – where, Paul happened to know, Michael always kept a bottle of poteen 'for emergencies' – was polished until its tin sides glowed.

To Paul's horror, all this looked as if a hurricane had hit it. Michael's garden – his pride and joy – had been trampled underfoot. Vegetables had been uprooted – there was a positive mixed salad of onions, potatoes, and cabbages everywhere. The flower pots had been hurled from the window ledges and smashed to pulp. Scarlet petals were scattered like confetti across the yard. The usually limpid waters of the duck pond had been stirred by its flustered occupants into soup, while the hens were all gathered on a branch of the apple tree gawping at their hen-house down below. Little wonder! For the roof looked as if an elephant had sat on it, and the door, half off its hinges, swung, creaking dismally. Rosy the donkey, wearing the broken gate of her paddock like a collar, was giving voice to her complaints as only a donkey can. Beside the badly scratched blue door, the upset milk churn was rocking like a demented cradle, and had it not been for the noise the animals were making, one would have heard the poteen bottle rattling in its depths.

The apparent perpetrator of all these crimes was standing on his hind legs with his front trotters halfway up the wall of Michael's house. His corkscrew tail was twisting in and out of sailor's knots, his black ears were working like two turbines; he was screeching like a chain saw. Michael, his moon face the colour of ripe plums, was standing in the

middle of his ruined garden throwing onions, cabbages, potatoes – whatever he could get his hands on – at something on the roof.

'Come down out of that, ya thief, ya vandal ya!' he was bellowing, 'before me chiminy's broke!'

'I will not.'

Pacifus, pale even for a ghost, sat astride the roof ridge. One arm was clinging to Michael's stovepipe chimney like a clamp. With the other, he was clutching something hidden at his chest. 'I'm staying put until you call that heretical animal off,' he vowed.

'Heretical animal!' Michael danced a jig on a newly planted row of carrots. 'Sure, the poor creature only wants what's his. He found it, hidden in the hedge. He has a right to keep it. It's his feeding bowl, I tell you.'

'Feeding bowl be tinkered!' Pacifus vanished and reappeared in quick succession. Dot-dot! Dash-dash! Like a message flashed in Morse. When at last he settled into visibility, his sleeve slipped back to reveal what had been hidden from Paul's view. It was the chalice! 'Hey, give me that,' he cried, joining Michael in the garden.

It took some time for tempers to be soothed, wounded pride mended, and Pacifus coaxed down from the roof. He refused to stir until Tantony had been led away, to be consoled by a heap of broken vegetables in his trough. Even then, pig and monk continued to eye each other suspiciously, small black eyes and large blue ones exchanging wary glances. Uprighting the milk churn, Michael delved for the poteen bottle, and took a long medicinal swig. Explanations followed.

It seemed that, like Paul, Michael All-alone had got up early that morning. As it promised to be a fine day, he and Tantony decided to go 'rootling'. Rootling, Michael explained, was something Tantony did particularly well. 'He *finds* things,' he told them, gazing lovingly at the pig's broad back and busily chomping jaws. 'They turn up for him.' (Indeed, Michael's small house was stuffed with such trophies!) They had not been rootling for long when the chalice 'turned up' in the hedge.

'It was so beautiful,' sighed Michael. 'He was so proud of it, I thought I'd let him keep it.'

Returning home in triumph, they had filled the chalice with porridge and potato peelings, and because the porridge was still too hot to eat, had left it on the window ledge to cool while they went out to rootle some more. On this occasion they had met Paul and Pacifus. It was while Michael was proudly showing the admiring ghost round his small domain that disaster struck .... Tantony had been found with his nose in the chalice, happily munching his potatoes and porridge. Indignantly, Pacifus had snatched the pig's breakfast from under his tip-tilted nose ... with terrible results.

'I see now I made a mistake,' Michael admitted. 'I should have known a classy bit of silver like that was bound to belong to someone. The trouble is,' he turned to Pacifus, 'if you're going to stay here, you can't have that thing. 'Twould make Tantony terrible jealous.'

'That's no problem. I can keep it.' At last, Paul thought, things were going his way. Accepting no arguments, he tucked the chalice underneath his arm, whistled Bess, and without a backward glance marched off towards the farmhouse. It was only as he was rounding the corner of the haggard that he remembered the gardai! Raising her hackles, Bess growled a warning. Parked in the centre of the yard stood a squad car.

Hand on Bess's ruff to silence her, Paul backed into the shadows of the hay barn. Flat on his stomach – Red Indian style – he made his way by a roundabout route towards the back door, using the farm out-buildings for cover. Stiff and important at the driving wheel, the officer did not pay him any heed. Even when Paul disturbed one of the farmyard cats, sending her streaking right in front of the parked vehicle, he did not turn his head. There remained a few more yards – in the open, with nothing to shield either him or the glittering chalice from view, both from the windows of the house and from the car itself. Paul was just debating whether he should try throwing a stone to divert the officer's attention while he made a quick dash for it, when he noticed a side door, leading to the fruit garden and Mrs. McQuaid's wash line, left wide open. With relief, he ducked behind a row of black currant bushes, and bolted into the house.

His problems were not over. No sooner had he reached the passage on his way to the kitchen, than his ear caught the sound of men's voices, and heavy feet approaching. Choosing the first door he came to, he slipped inside.

The room was a boxroom, used for storing anything not in immediate use. Spying an old tin trunk, Paul raised the lid and popped the chalice inside. He remained where he was, sitting on the lid of the trunk, until he judged the coast was clear. Leaving the chalice in its hiding place, he walked with a studied air of innocence along the passage to join some students drinking coffee in the kitchen.

CHAPTER 9
AN ODD CATCH

The next few days were surprisingly uneventful. Almost dull! Grandfather was called suddenly away to Dublin on University business. He left unexpectedly, huffing and gruffing that the students would be incapable of mending the dig or sorting out what could be salvaged from the smashed artifacts without him. Paul missed his opportunity to deliver the chalice into his hands, together with a speech he had prepared specially for the occasion. He consoled himself with the fact that his grandfather would soon be back. In the meantime, the chalice was quite safe hidden in the trunk.

To his relief, the attention of the gardai had moved away from the farm and its surroundings. Vincent had vanished. A nationwide police alert was failing to find him. His followers, rounded up and brought in for questioning, were as bewildered as everyone else. They swore they had never touched the amber. All they could say about their leader was that he had gone off on his bike, alone. None of them knew where. Unable to pin any evidence upon them, the gardai were forced to let them go.

It would be wiser, Paul decided, to let Pacifus and Michael settle their differences over Tantony without his interference. He avoided Michael's smallholding, occupying his time helping the students at the dig. During the first few hours he found himself glancing frequently over his shoulder, but as time went by, and no Viking warrior crept up behind, he forgot about visitors from the Past and concentrated upon the job at hand. He found nothing of any interest.

After three days of fruitless excavation he grew weary of archaeology. He decided to take the next day off, to go and visit Michael All-alone and Pacifus.

He found the smallholding somewhat quieter than when he had been there last. Tidier, too. The yard had been swept thoroughly, the geranium pots replanted, the garden raked, and all the fences mended. Rosy was nodding peacefully behind a brand new gate, the ducks preened their feathers by the still waters of the pond, and the hens were scratching contentedly for grain beside their patched-up hen house. Loud snores, coming from the pigsty, announced that Tantony was taking his midmorning nap. There was no sign of the owner of the place, nor of his guest. A piece of paper pinned to the newly repainted door informed Paul they had 'Gon Fishin'.

Under the mis-spelt words there was a second message, in flowery letters of purple, green, and red, with a serpent curling round the capital. Very pretty, but unreadable, for it was in Celtic miniscule. As Paul struggled to make it out, the letters melted, leaving the lower half of the paper blank. Chuckling, he went down to the river.

The pair – now apparently the best of friends – were happily engrossed upon the bank; Michael was busy casting flies, and Pacifus, wearing Michael's wellingtons (which were far too big and made him look like a performing sea lion, but which he said were essential as nowadays it was 'dangerous' to get his feet wet) was jumping about waving the landing net, and offering advice.

It was pleasant by the river, with the bees buzzing amongst the flowers on the bank, and an early swallow dipping low over the pool where the two were fishing. Paul caught a glimpse of electric blue as a kingfisher – more painted yo-yo than bird – dived from the willows and returned in one swift movement. He sat down upon the grass to watch the action.

Michael's line whined as he cast it out, the reel whirring as it spun. After a while the line went taut. The rod, bending like a bow, started to quiver. 'He's caught something,' Pacifus announced unnecessarily, bouncing up and down in his big boots. 'Looks like a large one. I wonder if it's that old trout that I used to .... Play him carefully now, Michael. Don't let him go, boy. I have the net ready.'

'I can't,' snarled Michael, desperately trying to wind the reel and failing. 'The line is stuck. I don't think it's a fish, at all.'

'Bring it in gently. Don't jerk, or you'll break the line.' Paul was on his feet, also offering advice. All at once whatever it was gave way, and Michael, arms and legs windmilling in an effort to stay upright, fell back with a splash into the water.

'He's soaked me! I'm all wet. I'll melt!'

'Nonsense! Of course you won't.' Paul snatched the net from the protesting ghost. 'Can't you see he needs our help? He's caught something very odd.' Kicking off his trainers, he plunged into the river.

What came up in the landing net was odd indeed! Long, and heavy, encrusted with rust .... And definitely *not* a fish.

'Janey-mac! What is it?' River water dripping from his clothes, Michael gaped at the thing they had pulled on to the bank. His hook had become embedded in a crossbar at one end. Taking out his knife, he cut the line.

'I'm not sure. I think ....' Something at the back of Paul's mind told him he had seen the object once before. He borrowed Michael's knife and scraped away at some of the rust. It came away quite easily, pattering to the ground like drops of scarlet rain to form a patch that looked unpleasantly like blood. What had seemed to be a knobbly iron bar began to take new shape. Hilted at one end, pointed at the other. 'It's ...!'

Dropping Michael's knife, Paul backed away. He knew exactly what it was, and where he had seen it last! His work had begun to reveal a pattern – very faint, and in some places worn off altogether, but there could be no mistaking it .... A pair of dragons writhing on a blade. When he had seen them last they had been flashing in bright sunlight on a long-gone morning, upon Ulfberht Longarm's sword!

'There's – blood – on – my – hands ...' The cry was no more than a whimper on the wind. 'Look at the monk!' screamed Michael. 'He's fading away. I can hardly see him.'

It was true. Soon all that was left was a pair of boots standing on the bank. After a moment's hesitation, the boots turned and moved hastily upstream – apparently on their own!

'My boots! My waders!' All Michael could do was gape at them, eyes boggling.

'It's the sword that's doing it,' Paul said, by way of explanation. 'Ulfberht Longarm's sword. Pacifus thinks he killed him. It makes him feel guilty. Go after him, will you? Tell him it isn't true. See that he doesn't come to harm. I'm going to throw this back.'

'No, you're not. I'll not have that thing polluting the water and poisoning the fish.' Caught between his concern for his boots – disappearing fast – and his concern for the condition of the river, Michael grabbed the sword. He looked as if he was about to chase Pacifus with it in his hand.

'Don't be silly. It's been there for centuries, and the fish are thriving.' Paul snatched it back. He did not want to hold the thing for fear of what it might bring with it. He dropped it at once as if it was red hot.

The sword lay between them on the bank. What else might the river contain, Paul wondered? The Viking's bones? His winged helmet and coat of mail? He shuddered. 'What shall we do with it?' He spoke in a whisper.

'How would I know?' Michael was sulky. This was not one of Tantony's 'rootlings', and he did not want it. Besides, by now his boots were out of sight and he was worried. 'Give it to your grandfather,' he said sarcastically. 'He likes ould things from the Past.'

'I can't. He's gone to Dublin.' Panic was rising.

Michael scratched his head to give his brains a stir. His eyes travelled anxiously upstream to where his boots had vanished. 'Bring it to my Gran, then,' he said impatiently. 'She's a Wise Woman. She'll take care of it.'

Thrusting the object into Paul's unwilling hands, he sped off after his invisible friend ... *and* his boots.

CHAPTER 10
A VISIT TO A WITCH

Left alone, Paul weighed the heavy object in his hands. Now that Michael's back was turned, he might just as well throw the thing back into the river; he would never know. Curiosity got the better of him.

'A Wise Woman,' Michael had called his Gran. Paul knew what that meant. Local gossip had it she was a witch; Michael was always boasting of her powers. A Wise Woman! He had never visited a witch before. And wisdom was certainly needed ... if not for the matter presently in his hands, at least for certain other matters. Shouldering his burden, Paul took the route to the witch's cottage.

He went cautiously, partly because he was frightened the ghost of Ulfberht Longarm might suddenly appear to claim its sword, and partly because he was not sure how you addressed a witch when you met her first. If he got the formula wrong would she turn him into a frog, he wondered? He was comforted by the knowledge that Mrs. McQuaid visited the old lady from time to time, whenever a calf fell sick or the hens refused to lay. Indeed, it had been Mrs. McQuaid who had rescued Tantony – then the puny runt of the litter – naming him after St. Anthony's pig, and taking him to Michael's Gran when the vet said there was no hope and better to let him die. Look at him, now! But, Paul thought, shifting the position of the sword to ease a growing pain in his shoulder, Mrs. McQuaid was made of stronger stuff. Also, he recalled, whenever she went to see the witch she brought a gift. 'What do I have?' he said to himself. 'A rusty old sword ... probably followed by a ghost! She's not going to thank me for either.'

If Michael's cottage was the model of neatness – fit to win a 'Tidy Towns' competition on its own – his Gran's was quite the opposite. Standing at the gate, it was impossible to see the house for the wilderness growing all around, threatening to drown the roof in a sea of honeysuckle, rambling roses, vines, and brambles. A corkscrew of smoke curled out of the tangle, wavering this way and that as if uncertain of the direction of the breeze. It looked a funny colour, confirming Paul's worst fears (he was beginning to wish he had not come after all). An ancient rowan tree rustled its leaves in warning as he placed his hand upon the latch.

The gate sagged on its hinges, opening to reveal the largest cat he had ever seen, seated on the mossy path. Paul hesitated. The animal before him was more like a tiger than a cat. Huge paw frozen in the midst of washing behind one tattered ear, it was fixing him with a malevolent green stare. Not the sort of cat to be called 'Pussy', while you stroked its arching back! For a long time Paul found himself mesmerised by two glittering points of green .... Then the cat blinked, releasing him. Contemptuously, it rose, and turning, led the way along the path. The tip of its orange tail twitched imperiously, and seemed to beckon. Obediently, Paul followed.

'What have you there? I can smell iron. Old, cruel iron. Why do you bring it to me?'

Paul almost dropped the sword. What he had taken for an old scarecrow behind a thicket of gooseberry bushes suddenly sprang to life. It burst through the thicket, heedless of the fact that it was leaving tattered ends of its clothes hanging on the thorns. 'Why bring it to me?' it demanded again, waving its tiny fists in the air. 'I don't like iron unless it's made into a pot. Iron destroys.'

'I – I'm sorry. I didn't know what else to do,' Paul stammered. 'Michael said ....'

'Michael? That one! What is the great baby up to now?' Michael's Gran could best be described as a bundle of rags. A colourful bundle, admittedly. A bright blue beret covered most of her wispy yellowish-white hair. For fear the beret might be blown off by the wind, which puffed and buffetted around her garden, she had tied a tartan scarf firmly over it, the ends dangling down to brush the yellow apron wrapped over her black coat. Black is usually dull and dreary, but Gran's black coat had been torn in so many places, and patched in so many different shades, it had become a garment for Harlequin to envy. Two more scarves – one bright scarlet, the other orange – were wound around her neck. To these she had added a Paisley pattern shawl, for at her age (which was at least a hundred) she had a dislike of draughts. A pair of stockings, handknitted in green wool, completed her attire. Her feet were thrust into a pair of rubber boots, cut low round the ankles and so scraped and threadbare, it was a wonder there was any waterproofing in them. Take away all these garments, Paul concluded, and there would not be much of the old lady left. The face and hands peeking out of the bundle were minute, shrivelled and wrinkled like dried-up kernels inside a nut. Her eyes, though, tucked into the cracks and folds of her face, defied her age. Black as jet like Michael's, they danced with life. They mocked him.

The cat mewed, impatient to continue his journey up the path.

'So you're inviting him in, are you?' his mistress asked. 'Well, I suppose you're right as usual. You leave that thing outside, though,' she said to Paul. 'I'm not having it in my house.'

'But ... *he* might come for it.' Automatically, Paul glanced over his shoulder. 'Him!' the witch scoffed. (She seemed to know who he was talking about.) 'You're surely not afraid of that long string of bones?

'Ah, not to worry,' she added more kindly. 'I've plenty of houseleek by the door. That'll fix him. *And* Thor, his noisy master.' Chuckling, she chose two fleshy leaves from the plant. She rubbed them on the crosspiece of the sword, and stuck it point first into a bed of marigolds. Wiping her hands on her yellow apron, she led the way indoors.

In contrast to the wind-tossed jungle of her garden, the inside of the witch's house was dim, and quiet, and almost bare. What furniture she had was plain and old. An oak settle and a rocking chair were drawn up to the smoky fire. There was a large dresser containing blue and white delft – most of it cracked or chipped. A wooden chest spilt its contents of clothes and blankets on the floor. A rickety ladder propped against one wall led to a loft, which acted, Paul supposed, as the witch's bedroom, for there was no sign of a bed in the only room downstairs. Caught between two worlds of light and shadow, for a while he saw everything through a haze of dancing rainbows and shooting stars. When the phantom colours faded, more homely details emerged – a kettle steaming gently on the hearth, a rush mat before the fire, handwoven baskets, patchwork cushions on the settle and chair. A sinister black pot on a pivot put him in mind of spells; but the smell coming from its bubbling depths was reassuringly familiar. Irish stew, he realised, sniffing with appreciation.

'Sit down, sit down. I'll make us a cup of tea.' The witch plucked two cats from the settle, dropping them unceremoniously upon the floor. As soon as Paul sat, they returned, curling up beside him as if what had happened was no more than a minor interruption to their shared dream. A small grey cat appeared from nowhere, and jumped upon his lap. There was no avoiding the creatures for they were everywhere – in the corners, on the dresser, halfway up the ladder, playing hide and seek amongst the tousled blankets by the chest. There was even a white cat curled up inside the bread oven in the chimney-place, while a large tabby sat purring beside her kindle of blind kittens in a basket by the fire. The orange tom – obviously the father – sniffed disdainfully at his squeaking offspring, before settling in a patch of sunlight near the door. 'Men!' sniffed the witch, passing Paul his cup of tea.

The tea tasted strange, like nothing he had ever drunk before. Paul sipped it doubtfully. Would it send him to sleep, he wondered? Give him nightmares? The aftertaste was surprisingly pleasant. Pepperminty ... with just a dash of orange! He took a longer gulp, and decided after all it tasted of chocolate. Looking up, he found the witch watching him. 'Well, why did you come? Tell me all,' she said, drinking her own tea with a loud slurp, and seating herself upon the rocking chair.

Hand stroking the drowsy cat upon his knee, Paul awkwardly began to tell his story. Once he had begun, he found the tale just flowed. Starting at the moment when he first saw Pacifus's face – big-eyed –

reflected in the glass at the museum, he went through every twist and turn, right up to the fishing of the sword out of the river , and Michael's boots running – apparently untenanted – along the bank. When he had finished, it felt as if a great burden had fallen from his mind. Putting down his empty cup he sat back, and closing his eyes, let the soft, neverending music of the witch's house take over.

Soothed by their mother's milk, the tiny kittens slept. Settled each in its own place, the older cats purred in unison. A chorus of purrs came from the dresser shelves, the rungs of the ladder, and wafted from the loft. Somewhere at the top of the chimney a pigeon cooed. The kettle hissed upon the hearth. Flames sucked the smoky turfs. The stew bubbled with a staccato beat. The witch's chair squeaked gently as she rocked it to and fro. 'Almost,' Paul thought sleepily, 'you can hear Time breathe.' He was jolted from his feeling of well-being by the witch's laughter. Like her eyes, her laugh was young.

'I'd say that you were haunted,' she remarked.

'I know. And it isn't funny.' Paul opened his eyes and glared at her. 'Just try it!'

'I have. I have.' The twinkle faded from the witch's eye. 'What do you think I can do?' she asked.

There came a tapping at the window pane. Paul shot a nervous glance in its direction, half-expecting to see a scarred weatherbeaten face leering at him from outside. There was nothing; only a rose branch knocking against the glass. Turning back, he met the witch's knowing look, bright as a bird's under the blue beret. 'People say you have ... magic powers,' he said haltingly. 'Michael's always boasting about it. I – I was wondering if you could weave a spell, or something. Maybe to keep Ulfberht Longarm out of the way .... At least until I have the chance to give the chalice back to Grandfather,' he finished lamely.

'Magic powers, is it?' the witch said quietly. 'Magic usually demands a price, you know. And ... when you've given the chalice back to your grandfather? What then?'

'What do you mean?'

'It seems to me, from your story, there will still be one or two pieces left lying about. What about your promise?'

'Promise?'

'To the little monk.'

'Oh, him! Well ... I didn't exactly ....' Paul's words trailed to silence. Pacifus's round face, blue eyes reproachful, swam before him. He groaned.

'As I said, you're haunted,' the witch chuckled, rocking in her chair. With a sudden slap, she brought both feet to the ground. Rising, she moved to the smoky fire and stirred it with her boot.

All sound and movement ceased. Pushed aside, the kettle and the pot fell silent. The feebly lapping flames sank to an amber glow. The cooing of the pigeon hushed. Beyond the window the wind died in the garden, and the rose hung limp against the frame. Curled heads in paws, the cats all slept. 'Time is holding its breath,' Paul thought, watching the bent form of the witch, gazing thoughtfully at the bright patch in the centre of the fire. He held his breath, also, not knowing what would happen next.

What followed was neither powerful magic, nor earth-shattering advice .... 'Rubbish!' the witch said sharply. 'Just a big fuss about bits and bobs that should have been left alone, that's all! Amber – Silver – Iron! Leftovers! What's so important about them?' She gave herself a shake, causing her colourful rags to flutter like a drift of butterflies disturbed upon a bush. At the sound of her voice, the cats opened their eyes. They yawned, and stretched and looked accusingly at Paul. 'You wouldn't say that if you'd had the amber burning in your pocket,' he said defensively. 'It dragged me back into the Past.'

'Back!' The witch seemed to find the word a joke. 'What would you say if I told you what you call "the Past", "the Present", and "the Future" all went the same way?' she challenged him. 'Just round and round, like tracks on a toy railway? You changed tracks, that's all. No harm in that. It's been done before. Occasionally, it's beneficial.'

'Oh, yes? I might have got stuck on the wrong track,' Paul said sarcastically.

'I doubt it. You were made to run on this one.'

Paul thought things over. 'Is that what's happened to Pacifus and Ulfberht Longarm?' he asked. 'Have they got stuck on the wrong track? If so, why? And when will they move back again?'

'When somebody changes the points, I suppose,' the witch said dryly.

'How? Can you ...?' The witch shook her head. She reached over and swung the arm of the pivot back into place. One drumbeat at a time, the stew began to simmer. The cats settled back to purr. 'Not my job,' she said briefly, and gave the stew a stir.

'Whose, then?' The witch cocked her blue-bereted head at him. 'You're the one who sees the ghosts,' she reminded him. 'I'm thinking perhaps it's yours.'

'But I can't. I don't know how ....'

'You'll find out sooner or later .... When stones begin to sing, I'm thinking. My grandson knows a thing or two about that. Perhaps he will help you. Meanwhile, you've a lot to learn, and some way to go, so you won't want to be weighed down by that ould thing in the marigolds out there. I'll tell you what I'll do. I won't use magic. As I said, magic requires a price and I don't think you're up to paying. But I will hide the sword until you need it.'

Paul had never heard of 'stones singing'. He was about to protest that the sword was not his, so he was never likely to need it. But it seemed the interview was over. Once she had made up her mind, the witch acted promptly. Letting go the ladle with which she had been stirring the stew, she grabbed Paul's hand, and with amazing strength for so small and old a woman, pulled him to his feet and led him back into the garden. Looking over his shoulder, he saw that the cats had all trooped out after them.

The wind had arisen again, stronger than ever. It whistled down the paths, buffeting the trees and bushes, and turning the leaves on end. Catching hold of Paul and the witch, it sent them spinning. It ruffled the fur coats of the cats and affected them with madness, so that they darted about, batting the nodding flower heads with their paws, pouncing on leaves, and chasing each other round in circles. 'Pay attention,' the witch called to them. 'I'll need your assistance.' Plucking the sword from the marigolds, she presented it to the reluctant Paul, and marched before him down the path. Suitably scolded, the cats fell into line and followed them.

The witch had said she would not use magic. But if what occurred was not magic, it was very like it.

On reaching the rowan tree by the gate the cats spread out to form a semi-circle. Seated, tails wrapped round paws, they faced the tree and began to purr.

As the purrs rose higher, spiralling upward like the smoke from the chimney, the witch added her voice to theirs in a long continuous hum. Wordless, but full of meaning, Paul thought, his ears ringing with the sound. Under the rowan tree, a strange thing began to happen.

All over the garden, the wind continued to buffet the plants. But in the shade of the old tree, everything became calm, and very still. Paul had the distinct impression that the rowan was listening. Slowly, imperceptibly, it began to lean towards them. Lower and lower, until Paul could feel its many-fingered leaves brushing his face. The cats fell silent. The witch ceased her song. 'Well, go on,' she urged in a hoarse whisper. 'She's asking for the sword. Don't keep her waiting. Give it to her.'

Paul stepped forward. For one foolish moment, recalling its beauty in the past, he thought he might like to keep the sword. But all the while it was growing heavier in his hands and he knew that sooner or later he would have to put it down, or drop it. Peering into the heart of the tree, he could see a deep, dark space, like a well, at the centre of its twisting stems; mossy and damp, smelling of rotting leaves and mould. Carefully, so as not to cut the living bark of the tree, he lifted the sword with both hands and eased it between the boughs. It fell into the space as easily as if it were entering the sheath on Ulfberht Longarm's belt, and vanished. Paul heard the leaves rustle, and felt once more the movement of the branches as the tree stood upright, and the wind returned.

'Well,' said the witch, wiping her hands on her flapping apron, 'that's that for the time being. A good job done, I'd say. I could do with a cup of tea.'

Without another word or glance at Paul, she turned, and followed by her train of cats (tails high, like banners of a triumphant army), re-entered her house.

CHAPTER 11
GONE!

When one had been expecting mumbled spells, evil-smelling brews, and dark dangerous happenings, it was all a bit of an anti-climax. For some time Paul wandered aimlessly. His steps took him back to the river but his friends were no longer there. Seeing the landing net abandoned on the bank, he picked it up, intending to take it straight to Michael. As he was passing the farmhouse, however, he swore he heard the witch's voice. 'The chalice! The chalice! Find the chalice!' It was so urgent, and sounded so close, he turned around, expecting to find her at his heels, she was not there.

'I haven't looked at the chalice since I put it in the trunk,' he realised. 'Perhaps I'd better do so.' Leaving the landing net propped against the wall, he went indoors.

Mrs. McQuaid was up to her elbows in flour, busy baking. She merely glanced up as he crossed the kitchen, and did not enquire what he was doing. 'Did you get your lunch?' was all she asked.

'No. I forgot.'

'Bless the child! Are you sick?'

'No. Just busy.'

'Ah!' Mrs. McQuaid was not one to question the young about their private concerns. She just nodded towards a tray of jam tarts. 'You'd better take a few of those to keep you going,' she said, and returned to pommeling dough.

Paul piled seven jam tarts one on top of the other in a sticky pyramid. Munching through the pyramid layer by layer, he went along the passage towards the boxroom. The door was wide open, which should have hinted to him that something was wrong, but with his mind on sweet warm jam and crumbly pastry, he sailed into the room unconcerned. For one moment he thought he had come to the wrong place, ... With the exception of a picture hanging askew upon the wall and a silent grandfather clock in one corner, the room was empty.

Everything else – including the black tin trunk – was gone!

'Mrs. McQuaid. Where is the black tin trunk that was in the boxroom?' Despite his efforts, Paul's voice quavered a little. Poised on the point of putting two soda cakes in the oven, Mrs. McQuaid looked up surprised.

'It's gone with the other old things to the saleroom,' she replied. 'There's an auction today, so Willie Rushe came yesterday with his van to collect them. Was there something in the trunk you wanted?'

'No - no. Not really. I – I just wondered,' Paul said. 'I have to go out for a while,' he added. 'I may be late back. If so, don't worry.' Leaving the kitchen in a hurry, he arrived at Michael's out of breath.

Michael, accompanied by a faint but slowly recovering Pacifus, had returned home. As his clothes were still wet he had changed out of them, into his only other suit. It was his best one! Paul found him looking uncharacteristically smart, wearing a bowler hat (a bowler hat, Michael considered, should always be worn with one's Sunday Best). He was putting up a clothes line in the yard.

When Pacifus heard the news, his recovery became immediate and complete.

'You can't be trusted,' he declared, swelling till he almost burst his habit with indignation. 'I knew I shouldn't have let that chalice out of my sight. What will Brother Gentilis think of this? As for Father Abbot ...!' Paul did not wait to hear what Father Abbot might have to say. He appealed to Michael.

'Where's the saleroom?'

When asked a sudden question, it took Michael some time to reply. He tipped up his bowler and scratched his head.

'''Tis a long way from here,' he said doubtfully.

'I'll get my bike, then.'

'I'm coming with you.' Pacifus was determined.

Michael scratched his head again. He came to what was for him a lightning decision. 'We'll all go,' he said, straightening his bowler. 'We can take the donkey cart.'

Rosy the donkey had other views upon the matter. But eventually she was persuaded that exercise was good for her, and allowed them to do up the straps and buckles .... Exercise is one thing. Too much exertion is another! Once on the road, she refused to go faster than a slow walk.

'Can't you move her on a bit?' Beside him, Paul could sense Pacifus getting fidgety.

'She'll go at her own pace, whatever.' Michael beamed lovingly at Rosy's flapping ears. He drove with the reins loosely on the donkey's back and the whip remaining in its stand, strictly for decoration. By the time they reached the saleroom the auction was over. There were just a few people lingering outside the warehouse, where it had been held, gossiping, or stowing purchases into vans, tying them onto the roof racks of their cars. 'Did you sell a black tin trunk?' Paul accosted an old man sweeping the floor inside the building.

'Which trunk would that be, now?' The old man took the pipe from his mouth, and leant upon his broom. 'There were several.'

'It was black,' Paul repeated, 'and made of tin. A bit battered. I think it had a label for Limerick Junction.' He racked his brains for anything else he might remember about the trunk.

'Ger! Did you sell a black tin trunk with a label for Limerick Junction?' the old man bellowed to a youth, who was sorting through some left-over items at the far end of the room. 'That went hours ago,' came the reply. 'It sold early. Went for peanuts.'

'Who bought it?' Paul was breathless.

'We do not divulge such matters. Our business is private and confidential.' The auctioneer's clerk had entered from the yard. He was a pasty-faced young man, his hair sleeked down with oil. A tongue of hair had broken loose to lick his pale forehead. He carried a clipboard, and oozed self-satisfaction.

'This is *very important*,' Paul insisted. The young man pursed his lips, and turned away.

'How can something be "private and confidential" at a *public* auction?' Paul exploded to the narrow back, busily bent over its accounts. There was no reply.

'I saw who got the trunk.'

The speaker was a red-faced man in a beer-stained suit, the sort of character often found 'looking on' at a country auction. He was leaning against the doorpost listening with interest to the conversation. ''Twas those two antiquey fellows from Ballinagad.'

'Mr Varnish and his friend. I know them.' The old man with the broom nodded. He cast a look at the clerk's bent back. There was something about that look that suggested shady dealings. Paul rushed back to his friends waiting in the cart.

'Michael, how far is it to Ballinagad?'

'Miles away. Near the sea. Rosy will never make it.'

'She'll *have* to,' Paul insisted between his teeth.

They drove in silence, broken only by Pacifus's sobs. Following a short tirade on the subject of Brother Gentilis, and what he would do to them if they did not recover the chalice (painful penances and the Fires of Hell loomed large!), he had turned tearful again. Michael sulked. Only once did he open his mouth, to inform them with injured dignity that the journey was too much for Rosy; she would 'break her feet'.

She did not 'break her feet'. She plodded forward until a large clump of thistles by the side of the way claimed her attention, and she refused to go further. Fortunately there was a signpost leaning drunkenly out of the thistles. 'Ballinagad 4kms,' it said.

'Leave her,' Paul said authoritatively. 'We'll walk.'

They wound Rosy's reins loosely round the signpost, and left her to munch her prickly feast while they marched on to Ballinagad. A tangy salt breeze blew in their faces, telling them they were nearing the sea. Above their heads, a gull whined like a fractious child. 'The wind is from the south,' Pacifus informed them. 'A white wind. That brings the Lochlannachs.'

'Oh, shut up about the Lochlannachs,' Paul said irritably.

Ballinagad, when they reached it, was a maze of a place; all winding streets and narrow alleyways. It seemed strangely empty. Most of the shops were already closing for the night. Enquiries about the antique shop brought only shrugs and odd looks.

Eventually they found the place almost by accident, at the end of a shabby rundown street. It was the last building on the block, almost falling off the row. It sold bric-a-brac rather than antiques, Paul decided, peering through the grimy window. A thin layer of dust and dead flies covered all. In the background strange shapes swathed in white sheeting gave the place a haunted look. 'I don't like it,' he heard Pacifus muttering beside him.

A creaking notice (much in need of polishing itself) above the door said:

MESSRS. WORMWOOD &
VARNISH
FURNITURE RESTORERS
FRENCH POLISHING
A SPECIALITY

'What odd names. I bet they're phoney.' Paul attempted to sound cheerful. He reached for the handle. The door was locked. The place was in darkness, but a slit of light from another door at the back suggested somebody was on the premises. An old van was parked by the kerb outside. 'You stay where you are,' he whispered to Michael. 'I'm going round the back to take a look.'

The faded wooden door into the back yard was also locked. Paul was forced to climb the wall, and knocked his shins. He envied Pacifus his ability to *plop* through bricks. The ghost emerged on the other side with no harm taken. The yard was littered with all kinds of odds and ends. Most of which had sharp corners to catch one in the gloom. Paul struggled

through and caught up with Pacifus at a lighted window. Ducking, he waited for a while. Then, cautiously raised his head, and peeped over the sill.

He found himself looking into a small square room, like a box. Perhaps it appeared smaller than it was because it was stuffed with wooden packing-cases, all piled high from floor to ceiling. The only remaining space was occupied by an expensive mahogany desk (highly polished), and a padded leather swivel chair. A tall metal safe was set against one wall. There were two men in the room, but Paul did not notice them at first. His attention was immediately riveted by the contents of the desk .... a telephone, a lighted lamp under a rose pink shade, a hideous bronze statuette, an enormous ashtray containing half a cigar (still smoking), a litter of catalogues and other papers, and

– at his elbow, Pacifus gave a little cry of pain – wreathed in the blue smoke of the cigar, its sides blushing pink beneath the lamplight, stood the chalice.

'Look at the smoke! It's burning. We must get it.'

'Oh, don't be so silly. How?' The window had thick bars over it. 'You're the one who can go through things,' Paul said sarcastically. 'Just slip between the bars and through the glass, and fetch it.'

'Can't,' Pacifus whimpered. 'The bars are iron. I don't go through iron. It gives me a headache.'

Paul was about to retort that in that case the chalice had better stay where it was, and that , if he had to be saddled with a ghost, why did it have to be a cowardly one? ... when the telephone on the desk rang shrilly, and a hand reached out from behind the packing cases.

It was a plump hand, very pink and clean with stubby fingers, one of them weighed down by a large signet ring. The arm which followed looked as if it had been poured into a sleeve that was so well pressed it must have creaked. An opulent cuff-link flashed on a stiffly starched shirt cuff. The hand hovered for a while above the desk before plumping down upon the phone and snatching the receiver from the cradle. A face appeared – oddly disembodied by the pile of cases – and the instrument was brought towards its ear.

'Varnish here,' wheezed the owner of the face.

Chapter 12
A Queer Pair Of Rogues

With much puffing and blowing, Mr. Varnish squeezed himself from behind the packing cases – like a wine cork eased gently from its bottle – and flopped down upon the swivel chair. Large though the chair was, Mr. Varnish fitted it well. He too was very large. Plucking the cigar from the ash tray, he popped it into his small round mouth and applied his ear once more to the receiver. 'Fire away,' he ordered through a billowing cloud of smoke.

Phoney or not, Paul decided, the gentleman's name suited him to perfection. From the top of his gleaming head (quite bald, not a hair upon it), down across his billiard-ball-smooth face and clothes, so tightly worn he seemed to have been sewn into them, to the very tips of his shining shoes, he had all the appearance of an advertisement for his own French polishing. 'Go on. I'm listening,' he wheezed, removing the cigar long enough to send a flight of smoke rings towards the ceiling.

At this, a second face appeared around another pile of packing cases. It drew after it a body as long and lean as Mr. Varnish's was short and stout. This person was definitely not French polished. Cobwebs were festooned on his ruffled hair, dust was smeared on his gaunt cheeks and on his high, worried forehead. Clutching a duster in his bony fingers, he strained with difficulty to listen to the conversation.

Like all conversations overheard by eavesdroppers, it was one-sided. Paul – ear pressed as close to the window as the bars would allow – could catch only, 'Yes ... Yes,' (delivered with a satisfied nod from Mr. Varnish's polished head) then, 'Tonight? We'll be ready.' This was followed, after a mischievous look towards his partner, by, 'Friend Wormwood has been busy. We've plenty for you. By the way,' here, he lowered his voice, and his plump hand came out to stroke the chalice, 'he's found you something rather special. We must discuss a price.'

'No!' Mr. Wormwood's shrill falsetto voice almost reached High C. His protest came too late. Already his partner had dropped the receiver to its cradle. Swivelling round, he folded his plump hands across a broad expanse of waistcoat, and stretching his short neat legs, eyed his companion wickedly through a smokescreen.

'But ... you promised. When I bid for that trunk, you said ....' Several packing cases crashed to the ground, as Mr. Wormwood tried to free himself.

'Ah now, Wormy! Let's be realistic.' Mr. Varnish's tones were as smooth as his appearance. 'This is no piece of Victoriana tat; no bit of tin dressed up to look like bronze. You can't keep this. While you were busy ...'

'Doing all the dusting and the sorting out,' Mr. Wormwood cut in indignantly.

'Just so. You keep the place beautiful, not a fingerprint on anything.' Mr. Varnish was oily in his effort to placate. 'As I was saying, while you were busy at your chores I was doing a little research. This thing, Wormy old lad,' he tapped the chalice, 'is worth a fortune. Just think! Only two others like it in the country. And they are both in the Dublin

Museum. No wonder the gardai are running round in circles! So we must get it out tonight, along with everything else, before they catch up with it. Oh ho, the Argies will pay well for this, I'm telling you.' He rubbed his fat hands with glee.

'But ...' Mr. Wormwood was forlorn. His partner was having no more nonsense. Stubbing out his cigar, he consulted a large fob watch on a chain. 'Time to get going,' he announced. 'We mustn't keep our contact waiting. And, just in case those twitching fingers of yours get too restless,' he added (for Mr. Wormwood had started woodenly to inch closer and closer to the chalice), 'I think we'll put this thing under lock and key while we're packing up the van.'

So saying, he whipped the chalice from under Mr. Wormwood's nose, and took it to the safe. His stubby fingers deftly worked the knob, and the heavy metal door swung open. Triumphantly, Mr. Varnish placed the chalice in the dark depths of the safe. Ears strained, Paul and Pacifus heard the lock click to as he closed the door upon it.

'I have an uncle who can break into them things.' Michael's voice caused them both to jump. Weary with waiting in the street, he had arrived behind them. 'But he's in gaol,' he added ruefully.

'Then he won't be much use to us,' Paul snapped irritably. 'By the time he's out the chalice will be in Argentina.'

'Where's Argentina? Is there such a place?' Pacifus's voice was weak. The combination of iron bars and iron safe was taking its toll, Paul noticed. He was beginning to fade away. Desperately, he turned to watch the pair of rogues shuffling and shunting their way out with the first of the packing cases.

'There's only one thing to be done.' Paul's decision was firm and final. 'We can't cope with this ourselves,' he told the others. 'I'm going for the guards.' Instructing Michael to keep the ghost as far away from the damaging effects of iron as possible, emphasising that they *must* stay hidden, he shinned up the wall and dropped silently into the street. As luck would have it, the dealers' backs were turned to him. He crept away.

He had some difficulty finding a phone box that was working. The message he gave was brief and to the point, but urgent. He had the odd impression the guard at the other end was expecting it. 'Go back to the shop but stay out of sight,' he was told. 'Whatever you do, don't try to tackle them yourselves. Those men are dangerous. We'll be round immediately.'

With a sigh, Paul replaced the phone. Deep down inside he had the uncomfortable feeling that he was letting down Michael's Gran. 'What else could I do?' he asked the stagnant air of the phone box, and thought he heard her snort of ridicule. What Pacifus would do once the chalice was in police hands he did not dare to think. In a gloomy mood, while he was in the phone box he decided to let Mrs. McQuaid know he was safe.

His garbled tale that he and Michael had gone for a trip to the sea, that Rosy had cast a shoe, and that they would probably have to stay overnight, drew some surprise. But he managed to convince the good lady he was not starving – they were near the sea, wasn't there a grand fish and chip shop? Putting down the phone, he was reminded that apart from a few jam tarts he had eaten nothing since breakfast. Feeling empty, he went to turn the lie into reality.

The shop was not as 'grand' as he reported. But he managed to buy a good supply of whiting fried in batter, plus a bag of chips for Michael (it was no use getting anything for Pacifus, he supposed. Ghosts, he had come to the conclusion, lived on air). He was late, therefore, getting back to the shop. In time only to see the tail- lights of the dealers' van disappearing down the street. Michael was standing on the empty pavement, open-mouthed.

Alone!

'Where's Pacifus?'

'Gone. He went with them.' Michael brushed aside the bag of chips.

'What do you mean, went with them?'

'Just that! They finished loading up the van with all them boxes, and the room was empty. The fat man went to the safe for the chalice. Then there was a terrible row. The thin fella was all for keeping the chalice to themselves – he's a bit of a collector, do you see? Has a place somewhere, where he keeps what he calls his "treasures". He wanted it to go there. The fat fella said no. Did he need his pin head examined? The chalice was too hot to hold, they would both end up in the clink. Anyway, think of all the money .... I didn't hear the rest of the argument, for at that moment Pacifus said he was feeling faint, and could we please go back to the street? The fat man must have won, though, for when we came round the corner there they both were, getting into the van ... with the chalice. As they drove off, Pacifus gave a sort of strangled cry and ran after them. He just melted through the back door. That was the last I saw of him.'

This was terrible! As Paul was trying to digest the news, the squad car drove up beside them, and the driver leant out of the window. 'Which way did they go?'

'That way.' Paul pointed along the street.

'To the coast, is it? We thought that would be their route.' The officer issued instructions through his microphone. 'They have been under suspicion for some time,' he explained to Paul. 'Smuggling stolen antiques to South America. We've had our eye on them of course, but they're crafty devils. At last, thanks to you, we may get the chance to catch them at it.' Already, the squad car was beginning to slide away. 'Wait,' pleaded Paul. 'Please take us along. You see, the chalice comes from our museum. It was my grandfather, Professor Sheean, who found it. Also –' He was reluctant, but he would have to tell them. 'They've kidnapped a friend of ours.'

'Kidnapping, is it? This is serious.' Hurriedly, the officer spoke into his microphone, sending the information to the other cars. 'I suppose you'd better come along,' he said doubtfully. 'Stay in the squad car, mind. And keep low. If you don't do as you're told, your friend's life could be put in danger.' Hardly likely, Paul thought wryly! Assuring Michael (always suspicious of the Law) he was *not* being arrested, he placed the bag of chips firmly in his hand and shoved him into the car.

They drove off at speed. Paul, clinging to the back seat, soon began to regret his mention of Pacifus, for the gardai demanded a full description of his friend, and wanted to know how he had been taken. 'He – he's a monk,' he faltered. 'I – I don't know how it happened, exactly. I wasn't there. He – he's very attached to the chalice, so perhaps it wouldn't let him go .... I mean, *he* wouldn't let *it* go,' he added hastily.

By now, they had left the town and were following a winding road towards the coast. The few remaining fields had given way to a broad expanse of marsh – lonely and featureless, except for the occasional pale gleam of water, like spilt buttermilk in what remained of the twilight. Somewhere, a solitary bird called plaintively. To their left, Paul could make out two tiny spots of light creeping like glow-worms across the flat grey landscape. Away to their right, another pair kept pace with them. 'Isn't it exciting?' he whispered to the munching Michael. 'Just like on T.V.' – forgetting Michael did not own a set as his Gran did not approve. She said they 'blurred vision'.

'That's them!' The officer in the passenger seat pointed to a pair of tail-lights, some way ahead, jumping and bouncing whenever the van met a bump in the road. 'They're heading for the flat ground of the cliff top,' commented their driver. 'Just right for a landing. Here comes the plane. Look!' A shape had appeared in the sky above the sea. It was no larger than a bee, but growing rapidly bigger as it approached. Lights winked on its undercarriage as it began to circle ... 'Pull up and wait. Switch off all car lights, we'll take them by surprise,' ordered the officer at the microphone.

They sat, and waited. The gardai spoke to each other in low undertones. Now and again the microphone crackled, and another voice – tinny – joined the conversation. Michael continued, stolidly, to munch. Paul held his breath. He could hear the drone of the aeroplane, drawing nearer. Altering course, it was now following the coast. 'Has he spotted us? Is the game up?' The officer was growing uneasy. 'No, it's all right. He's coming in. We'll let him land. Allow them to start the loading ... Now!'

Orders were barked over the microphone. Lights blazed. Sirens wailed. The short distance to the cliff top seemed to be covered at a leap. Paul was flung against Michael, the remaining chips went everywhere. They clung together in a greasy tangle as the squad car left the road and bounced across the grass. Other cars drew up beside, all swerving to a halt ....

'Garda! Garda! Don't move. You're under arrest.' The voice of an officer blared through a megaphone.

Caught in the midst of unloading the van, poised in the glare of the headlights (nowhere to go but the steep cliff beyond), Messrs. Wormwood and Varnish were like actors on a well-lit stage. Mr. Wormwood dropped the packing case he was carrying, on his toe. Jerkily, he raised his hands in a gesture of surrender. The fake jewels on his partner's cuff-links flashed, as he covered his face to shield it from the light. There was a third man – from the plane – a small, sun-tanned foreigner, frozen stiff as a guardsman. 'Put up your hands,' the officer called to him. 'Stay where you are,' he ordered Paul and Michael. The gardai leapt from their vehicles.

At this, there came a swirl of movement from the actors on the *stage*. Mr. Varnish attempted to creep away (only to find himself in the strong arm of the Law, protesting his innocence), Mr. Wormwood flung himself squeaking with terror full length on the ground; with a sudden gesture the foreigner appeared to raise his hands, then dived into his pocket for a gun. The gardai reached for their revolvers, and the shooting began ... 'Janey!' gasped Michael. He dropped onto a pile of cold chips on the floor.

'Where's Pacifus in all this?' Paul wondered frantically. The van doors were wide open, but there was no sign of him. All at once, he spotted a movement amongst the packing cases. Chalice hugged to his chest, Pacifus was scuttling to and fro like a frightened rabbit. 'Pacifus! Here!' Paul shouted. Heedless of the gardai's warnings, he jumped out of the car.

A burst of firing came from the plane. The pilot was armed with an automatic shot-gun. Squealing with terror, Pacifus leapt into the air. Still clutching the chalice he began to run as fast as his sandalled feet would take him, away from the headlights and the noise. 'Wait!' screamed Paul, running after him.

More firing! They kept running. Paul was sure he heard a bullet whistle past his ear, scudding into the soft grass of the cliff top. By now they were beyond the lights. The change to his sight had him stumbling over tufts of thrift, twisting in the shallow scrapes left by rabbits. To his relief, the moon rose. Round and full. He was able to see Pacifus – still racing ahead, his feet seeming to skim the moonlit grass. 'Wait for me,' he gasped ....

His voice was drowned by a roaring from the plane.

Abandoning his cargo and his passengers, the pilot had taken off and was heading out to sea. Caught in the flight path, all Paul could do was fling himself face down upon the ground. The noise was deafening. The plane seemed to pass over him with barely a foot to spare; Paul could feel the cold gush of its afterdraught along his back .... Quite suddenly, all sound was cut off. Completely. As if somebody had closed a padded door. 'The engine has stalled. The plane is going to crash,' Paul thought. Paralysed by terror, he waited for falling debris to land upon his head.

Nothing happened. For a long time Paul lay still with the silence hanging round him like a heavy curtain. Gradually, he became conscious of the dampness of the sea-sprayed turf seeping through his clothes. He dared to move.

Overhead, the stars were twinkling in the sky. To either side stretched the clifftop, serene and untroubled in the moonlight. All was very quiet and still. The same unearthly stillness, Paul realised, he had experienced once before, when he had gone back in time, in the Quarry field, close to Kilcarrigan Abbey. He looked about. There were no shouting, struggling men. No gunshots. No squad cars. No gardai. Only a long line of standing stones – like those he had dreamed about in his tent – casting black shadows on the close-cropped turf. Leading in a straight line towards the cliff edge, and the murmuring sea.

Paul found himself shuddering. Just like in his dream, Pacifus was running between the line of stones. To Paul's horror, it seemed he could not stop. Just where the last pair of stones met the cliff edge – slanting slightly because of the wave-worn ground beneath – the avenue continued and changed to a silver road cast by the moon upon the water. Halfway down this road, riding at anchor, its square sail furled, its oars dripping moonlight, the dragon-headed prow dipping and bowing to the waves, was a Viking longship! 'Pac – i – fus!' Paul started forward. As he crossed the black bar of shadow thrown by the first stone something leapt out at him. There came a heavy crunch upon his skull. It made him see lights ....

'... But not angels!' he thought dimly, recalling Pacifus's story as he pitched forward into darkness.

CHAPTER 13
THE AMBER IS RETURNED

Michael All-alone was feeling miserable. Miserable and, unusually for him, lonely. He did not know where his friends had gone. And he had just spent several hours – together with Mr. Wormwood and Mr. Varnish – in police custody, unable to answer the gardai's questions.

How long had he known Messrs. Wormwood and Varnish? Alias, Smith and Jones? More correctly, Murphy and O'Reilly? When, exactly, had he become their accomplice? ... Michael had shaken his bowlered head. He had never heard of half these people. He did not understand the meaning of the word 'accomplice' .... Where was the boy? Where was the monk he had mentioned? Did he exist at all? For that matter, where was the Kilcarrigan Chalice?

Again, Michael shook his head. Taking off his bowler, he ran his fingers through his springy heather hair. He did not know the answers to the questions. He wished he did.

Snapping his biro with frustration, the officer interviewing him heaved a sigh. 'Detain those two,' he said, pointing to a cringing Mr. Wormwood and a blustering Mr. Varnish. 'Find me an interpreter so I can understand what that jabbering Argentinian says. You can let this one go,' he indicated Michael. 'We've nothing on him.'

Put out in the street, Michael wandered round Ballinagad for more than an hour hoping Paul and

Pacifus would come back to him. They did not. He was cold and tired, his feet hurt. What was worse, the chips had given him indigestion .... Then he remembered Rosy!

'The poor old ass. She'll be lonely, too,' Michael said to himself. 'Well, as that other pair seem to have gone off gallivanting, she and I might as well go home together.' Finding the route out of town, he started along it. After a weary trudge, he came to the signpost. He knew it was the right signpost for it said 'Ballinagad 4kms', and it was leaning drunkenly. Something was missing. Michael peered at it in the moonlight. There were no thistles. There was no donkey cart .... And there was no Rosy!

'Somebody's stolen me ass!' Michael gazed this way and that along the deserted road as if he expected the thief to come and give himself up. There was nothing for it but to walk home. Perhaps, if he was lucky, he could thumb a lift.

He walked about half a mile. Nothing came. Ballinagad was not the sort of place where people held parties late into the night; there was no one returning home after an evening of enjoyment. He had walked a full mile, and was just beginning to think of bedding down in the ditch for the night to wait to catch the milk lorry in the morning, when he heard the distant sound of an engine on the road behind him.

'At last!' Michael positioned himself in the middle of the road so he would not be missed, and stuck out his thumb in the well-known signal. 'Don't be thumbing lifts,' his grandmother was always telling him. 'It's dangerous.'

'Sure, it can't be helped,' Michael said to himself. 'This is an emergency.'

The vehicle was drawing nearer. By now Michael could tell by the sound it was only a motorcycle, but at least, he told himself, it was better than nothing, and he could always ride the pillion. He began to have doubts when the motorcycle came into view. It was, even in Michael's inexperienced opinion, behaving very oddly.

One minute, it was forging straight ahead .... The next, it had turned tail, and was travelling away again. Back it came .... Only to change its mind and repeat the odd performance! Now, it was approaching in a 'Will I? Won't I?' fashion, the engine spluttering and choking, and the machine jumping like a kangaroo.

Gaining momentum, it bore down upon him. Michael was forced to jump aside. 'Are you trying to kill me?' he gasped, as it sped past showering him in a hail of tarry chippings. No sooner had he regained his balance than it was back again, swerving just in time and missing him by inches. 'You're drunk, that's what you are,' he shouted after it.

'Wait!'

As if infected by the same madness, Michael started to pursue the bike. In that brief instant as it had passed him by he had recognised the rider. Skull and crossbones blazoned on his chest! A wisp of long blonde hair whipping out from underneath the helmet! Not one of Michael's favourite people, but at least someone from nearer home. 'Hey, Vincent!' he shouted. 'Stop your fool-acting and give us a lift. Don't you know the police are after you?'

The motorcycle turned. The rider seemed to be struggling with it, but at least he approached at a more respectable speed. With some difficulty he raised his visor. It was Vincent all right but a Vincent who was greatly changed. Gone was the usual mocking leer; there was no hint of malice in his eyes. Certainly, he was not drunk. But he looked exhausted. Deathly pale. Terrified. And, Michael thought puzzled, strangely humble. 'What's up with you, Vincent?' he started to ask .... But once again the motorcycle took over.

With a rattling shudder, as if it was about to shed its nuts and bolts upon the road, it wheeled around. Despite Vincent's attempts to apply the brakes, it tore off bucking like a bronco. Michael watched it zig-zagging dangerously from side to side. 'I don't think Vincent is in charge of that machine at all,' he said to himself, taking off his bowler to scratch his head. 'It's more like it's in charge of him.' The machine did not return. Rounding a corner, it disappeared from view. The next thing Michael heard was an almighty crash, as if dozens of pots and pans had fallen from a shelf. 'Oh, my gosh!' he cried, running to the rescue.

Round the corner, he came upon a sorry sight. Vincent's motorcycle was in bits, fit only to be collected for the scrap-yard. Pieces of metal were strewn about the road. The handle-bars were up a tree. One wheel was swinging gently from a telegraph pole, while the other – buckled beyond recognition – was wrapped around a post. Beyond in a field the engine, freed from its usual restrictions, still mumbled sadly to itself like a beast with colic. The rider was lying flat upon his back. Eyes wide open, staring at the sky. 'He's dead!' said Michael to himself. Clapping his bowler to his heart, he approached on tiptoe.

Vincent was not dead. As soon as Michael came up, he began chattering wildly, tossing his helmeted head this way and that, and beating the grass verge with his gloved fists. Michael found it impossible to catch all that he was saying, but one or two words kept being repeated more often than the others ... 'Mascot! ... Take it away.' Then, 'Him!! Don't let him near me,' uttered with glazed eyes and a shaking voice.

'I don't know what you're on about, Vincent,' he said timidly. 'Could you speak more slowly, please. My Gran's forever telling me I'm not too quick on the uptake.'

Vincent made a colossal effort. You could tell how colossal the effort was because his face – ash pale beneath the helmet – turned crimson. Eventually, he managed to heave himself with difficulty on to his elbows. 'The mascot,' he repeated hoarsely. 'It's – on – the – handlebars. Take it away before He comes again .... Please!'

At this last word – so strangely unlike his usual vocabulary – Vincent's elbows gave way, and he sank back motionless. Michael even dared to give the silent body a little prod. Vincent said no more, just gave a sigh and let his head roll sideways. Mascot? Michael looked around. Mascots took many forms. Lucky coins, horseshoes, teddy bears, and such! Black cats, sometimes. No. They were called 'familiars', he knew that because of Gran. He really must concentrate, he told himself.

Try to think. Vincent had mentioned handlebars. Where were they? Glancing up, he saw them hanging from the tree. There was something yellow in the middle. It caught the moonlight. 'Is that it, Vincent?' he asked pointing.

There was no reply. Peering at him, Michael saw he had fallen asleep. A wisp of blonde hair lay across his face. He looked very peaceful. 'I'll not disturb

him,' he decided. 'Poor fella looks worn out, he needs his rest.' Gently he removed the piece of hair from Vincent's eyes, and took off his helmet to make him more comfortable. He tidied the wrecked motorcycle off the road, so it would not cause an obstruction .... Then he went back to the tree.

The handlebars were well beyond his reach. Michael got a crick in his neck, just looking at them. To his surprise, however, at that moment the branch they were hanging on snapped, and they came tumbling down. It almost looked as if the branch had been burnt away, for the end was blackened. A drift of smoke curled upwards. How to get the amber off the handlebars? Michael put out his hand, and withdrew it. No wonder the branch had been burnt away. The amber was red hot!

'Heat from the engine I suppose,' Michael thought, sucking his smarting fingers. Being no mechanic, used only to a donkey cart, he knew no better (Paul could have told him otherwise of course, and warned him to take no further action. But he was not there). At last, with the help of a large spotted handkerchief (his grandmother always insisted he carried one), he was able to release the charm.

'Why, it's a little hammer!' Michael might be no mechanic, but he did know something about tools. 'Not much use.' He studied it. 'It's only a toy. It's made of amber.'

Amber! Michael screwed up his face, trying to remember something his grandmother – an expert on precious stones and metals – had told him long ago. 'It carries the power of the Sun,' she had said. 'Used properly, it will give you energy. If you've a long way to go, or a hard job to do, put a piece of amber in your pocket and you'll feel the difference.' 'I have a long way to go,' Michael said. 'What a bit of luck!' Smiling to himself, he wrapped the piece of amber in his handkerchief, and popped it in his pocket.

Almost at once, he did indeed 'feel the difference'! 'Begob, it works,' Michael cried joyously. The road had begun to stream beneath his feet, like one of those moving walkways you find at airports. In next to no time, he was recognising familiar landmarks – a well-known barn – a much-loved tree – the cottage of a neighbour – 'I'll be home in a jiffy,' Michael told himself. The Knocknafeeny mountains reared tall to his left, as he approached them. He was just beginning to picture in his mind his neat little house, the glad welcome from his animals, and such homely comforts as a nice soft chair, a warm fire, and a good hot cup of tea, when he realised to his horror that his feet were out of control!

'Not so fast,' he pleaded, for without any prompting they had put on a spurt. 'Wait a bit. My shoelace is undone,' he protested. Try as he might, he found he could not stop.

'Hey! That's the wrong way, I don't want to go up there.' Now Michael was really frightened. His feet had left the road, and were marching him along a track leading to the very heart of the Knocknafeeny Mountains. 'Don't go walking on the wrong side of the Mountain, Mickeen Og,' his grandmother had often warned him. 'You haven't the strength of mind for it. There's strange folk up there. Especially on the other side. The Old Men of the Mountains would steal you brains away, and you not looking – Mind you,' she would add, 'they'd have a hard time finding a brain in that fuzzy head of yours . All the same it isn't worth the risk, so don't be crossing the mountains, especially after dark ....' Here he was, well after midnight, under the light of the moon – always a time for magic ('I'll get moonstruck!' he moaned), climbing the Knocknafeenys with all the speed and agility of a goat ....'But it's not my fault,' he said aloud, for the benefit of anyone who might be listening. 'It's my feet that's doing it.'

Up and up! The moonlight showed a bleak landscape of frochan and heather; mile upon mile of it, with here and there the looming shape of a boulder, tall and unwelcoming as a fortress. Bracken fronds dripped moisture he was sure held poison. Heather clumps stravaiged the way with the vowed intent to trip him. Michael was becoming more and more weary, but if anything his feet were moving faster.

'Don't you feel the blisters?' he asked them. 'Why are you doing this?' Glancing up, he saw the answer.

A man was standing on the brow of the hill, very still in the moonlight ... and bright! Moonbeams glittered like frost on his winged helmet and coat of mail, and slid icily across the blade of the axe he carried in his hand. With his other hand, he was beckoning.

''Tis – one – of – those – Vikings the arkimelogical men let loose,' squeaked Michael. 'He's looking angry .... No, feet, no! Please don't go any further. Stop!!' His feet took no notice. He felt himself being dragged, like a trout he might have caught upon his line, nearer and nearer to the gleaming figure on the hill.

Now Michael began to fight – fight for his life, just like the fish upon the hook. 'If I ever get out of this I'll never catch another trout,' he vowed, twisting and jerking as he tried to free himself. The Viking flung back his head and laughed. His laughter echoed like thunder in the Knocknafeeny Mountains. Swinging his axe, he began slowly to descend.

'No! No!' Just like the fish landed on the bank, gasping for breath, Michael continued to struggle helplessly. His boots felt like they were clamped with iron, holding him in place. All he could do was twitch feebly, waiting for the Viking's axe to fall.

'Gran! Oh, Gran! I'm sorry I went up the mountains. I won't do it again. I promise. Please – help – me!'

It was a last desperate wail ... but it did the trick! As the Viking's axe came singing through the air, Michael found himself somersaulting backwards. Tumbling head over heels, like the proverbial stone gathering no moss, he went rolling downhill – faster and faster, until he landed against something very hard, and stopped. Breath knocked from his body, he lay still.

CHAPTER 14
PIRATES!

When at last Paul opened his eyes the sun was shining full on his face, dazzling him. Painfully he closed them again, and lay watching the red lights zig-zagging behind his eyelids while he tried to figure out what had happened. His head ached, and he found it hard to move. His feet and hands felt as if they had been glued together, and whenever he tried to turn his head something grabbed him by the throat and throttled him. There was an unaccustomed mix of noises: hisses, and creaks, and groans, while from overhead came a sharp slapping sound, as if someone was beating a heavy carpet with a stick. Through a rising wave of nausea, brought on by the constant swaying of the floor beneath him, came memory. And with it, understanding. He was aboard the Viking ship! Dreading what his eyes might meet, he opened them again, squinting sideways to avoid the light.

Pacifus was lying only a few feet away, flat on his back with his mouth open, on a pile of furs. Like Paul, he was bound hand and foot. There was a leather thong, rather like a dog collar, round his neck, from which a rope led to the tall mast with its flapping sail behind them. He looked very pale and still. 'Is he dead?' Paul wondered. 'No. He's a ghost, he can't be .... Pacifus,' he whispered softly, 'wake up. Can you hear me?'

Pacifus groaned. A suggestion of colour returned to his pale cheek. His eyelashes fluttered. 'Where are we?' he asked, half-opening his eyes. 'Oh! I think I can remember.' He shut them tight again.

'We're on the Lochlannachs' ship,' Paul reminded him. 'They must have caught us. Have you still got the chalice?'

'They're not Lochlannachs.' Pacifus's blue eyes shot open. The look he turned on Paul was almost comic. 'They're worse!'

'What do you mean, worse?' Paul fought with his bonds, trying to get a glimpse of the two rows of warriors at their oars on either side.

'Oh, good! You're awake!' The figure bending over him should have been a Viking. Indeed, it was dressed like a Viking, in helmet, leather jerkin, trousers, boots, and sword belt. But the voice! And the face underneath the helmet! Heart-shaped and smooth, with a dimple in its cheek. The eyes under their curling lashes were larger even than Pacifus's (they were bluish green). A pair of long auburn plaits interwoven with ribbon tickled his face as she leant close to him. 'Definitely not a Viking!' he thought, trying to sit up. 'She's much too pretty.' It was a woman!

'Girls! They're awake. Come and see.' The boat rocked violently as sixteen pairs of 'warriors' left their oars and scrambled for a view. There were cries of 'Ooh!' and 'Ahh!' and murmurs of 'God love him!' 'He's only a boy.' And, 'Isn't the little monk a dote?' (Pacifus shut his eyes tight again at this, screwing them up and turning pink in the face.)

'Don't push, you're upsetting the boat.' The young woman with the long plaits was obviously the leader. She clapped her hands. 'Back to your places,' she ordered sharply. 'Grania! Some wych hazel for the monk's poor head. A bottle of your special potion, too. They both look seasick.'

A trim elderly lady, her iron grey hair scraped back and tied in a neat plait, rose from her place by the big steering oar at the stern of the boat and advanced towards them. She was, Paul noted, the only member of the crew to wear a skirt. Regarding them with pursed lips, she produced a small earthenware bottle from a pouch at her belt and bathed Pacifus's head. A second bottle – well shaken – and a bone spoon delivered a dose of greenish liquid into his mouth. Pacifus fought against the treatment with clenched teeth, but his head was tipped expertly back, and he was forced to swallow. Paul received the same medicine. It tasted revolting, but made him feel much better. 'We'll soon be out of the choppy water,' Iseult, the young woman, told him (she was, she added for his information, a queen). 'Once we're round the point and into the bay it will be calm. We're making for the river mouth. Emer! Beat time, please. Row, girls. Row!'

A dark-haired girl (only a year or two older than Paul), with mischievous brown eyes and a mop of curls peeking out from under her helmet, picked up a bodhran, and started to play. The crew all pulled to the rhythm of her beat. 'Did you notice?' whispered Pacifus as soon as Queen Iseult, giving orders, moved to the bow of the boat. 'They're all ... women!' He blushed. 'Of course, I noticed,' Paul replied.

'Yes. But ... did you notice?' His voice sank even lower. 'They're all wearing ... breeches!'

'More practical, I suppose,' said Paul, watching the slim figure of Queen Iseult, feet planted firmly on the deck, braced against the heaving of the ship.

'Yes. Well ...' Pacifus shot her a disapproving glance from underneath his lashes. 'What are they all doing here, anyway? When they should be at home, doing the cooking and the spinning?' he demanded critically.

The answer was provided once they had anchored; the vessel hove to in a quiet backwater of the river, its dragon-headed prow wreathed in the willows of a leafy island. Reed buntings, disturbed by their arrival, lectured angrily from the rushes.

'Just the place for a picnic!' declared Emer, springing up and clapping her hands. She wore rather more jewelry than the others, and her necklaces and bangles clinked as she moved. She had embroidered forget-me-nots on her 'Viking' tunic.

'Sit down, and don't move till I tell you. You're rocking the boat,' Queen Iseult snapped. 'Fionnualla,' she turned to a brawny redhead, with freckles and an infectious grin, 'mind the prisoners. Maeve! Siobhan! Lower the mains'l. The rest of you ... unload the provisions.'

A great cheer went up as Maeve and Siobhan lowered the big striped sail, and laid it neatly on the deck. With a chatter of excited voices, bundles and baskets were passed overboard. Sticks were collected, and a fire lit with the aid of Grania's tinder box. A cloth was spread upon the ground. Paul and Pacifus felt themselves gripped by the large capable hands of the redhead and swung to the shore. 'What have you got under your habit?' Paul hissed, as his friend landed with a clank.

'The chalice.' Pacifus winked, and tapped the bulge. 'My wee bit of fishing net. Remember? It comes in useful sometimes.'

'I don't think this lot will steal the chalice,' Paul said. 'They're nice. I like them. Look at that feast!'

The ladies had been busy; the picnic looked delicious. There was enough food, Paul reckoned, to feed a whole fleet for a fortnight. 'But I can't eat like this,' he complained, sticking out his hands with his wrists bound together.

'Oh, sorry! That was Fionnualla's fault; she's a bit over-enthusiastic. It was she who hit you on the head, too.' Iseult produced a knife from her belt and cut them loose. 'Help yourselves,' she said.

'Have a honey-cake,' Emer offered Paul.' I made them specially. They're really sticky.'

'He must have a meat pie first,' Grania said severely. Although Queen Iseult was the leader of the expedition, it was the older woman – severe and straight-backed – who saw that the correct rules were kept. It was she who presided over the kettle (now bubbling merrily above the fire), and made sure the others had washed their hands in the river before laying out the food. It did not matter what he ate first, Paul decided, it all looked good. Leaning back against a willow trunk, he basked in the sunshine, the fresh air, the company, and the food.

If Paul received his share of spoiling, it was Pacifus – his chalice taken from him, admired, and set as a centrepiece on the cloth – who was given the greatest attention. The ladies flocked round him.

'Have a slice of my seed cake, Brother. It's a new recipe.' – 'More bread and butter?' – 'There's goat's milk cheese.' – 'There's heather honey.'– 'Have a little of both!' – 'A second cup of camomile tea? No trouble at all. I'll just top up the pot.' Grania beamed lovingly upon him. His 'fasting' friend, Paul remarked cynically, was tucking into everything with relish.

And lapping up the adoration of those beings, whom he had regarded with such suspicion and disapproval. He, himself, was feeling left out. 'Why did you take us prisoner?' he demanded, in order to gain attention (he had to repeat the question several times before anyone would listen!).

'All pirates take prisoners. It's part of their trade,' Queen Iseult explained. 'Grania thought you might be worth a ransom. Though, when she saw we'd taken a man of the Church, she felt rather guilty. She's very religious, you see. By then it was too late to put you back, for we were out to sea.'

'But why pretend to be pirates?' Paul persisted. 'Is it some sort of game?'

'This is no game,' Emer said indignantly. 'It's real. The men won't solve our problem, they're useless. Always too busy fighting amongst themselves.' She tossed her curls.

'It's the Lochlannachs,' sighed Queen Iseult. 'They've reached plague proportions on this coast.'

'They trample all over our gardens.' Grania was indignant. 'They steal the eggs,' (this from Maeve) 'and the chickens.' – 'They plunder the orchards.' – 'They kill our pigs.' – 'They burn our houses and barns.' – 'They take our friends as slaves ....' 'So,' Iseult finished triumphantly above the chorus of voices, 'after a storm, when we found one of their longboats on the beach, we decided to take matters into our own hands. We took it over.' – 'There were one or two of the crew left. Looking sick,' Fionnualla told him. 'I soon dealt with them. They're tied up with their own fishing lines. Neatly stacked in my cellar.' – 'Of course, our husbands were out on one of their silly little wars,' Emer added. 'We just left them a note telling them to get their own meals, and reminding them to look after the babies. Then, we came aboard .... I felt a bit seasick, at first,' she admitted, 'but I soon got over it. Now, I think it's fun!' She twirled in a dazzle of forget-me-nots and bangles.

'The only trouble is,' Queen Iseult laughed, 'since we took up pirating to sweep them off the seas, there hasn't been sight or sound of a single Lochlannach. Perhaps they're all afraid!'

Paul's mind travelled to the last time he had stepped into the Past (a more serious affair, altogether). He squinted up through the veil of willow leaves at the sun. Nearly midday! If what the witch said was true, that the two lines (Past and Present) ran parallel, moving together round and round, then his moment of arrival was just a matter of chance. The place, and the people he met were determined, it seemed, by where he was when the shift took place, but the actual moment was more subtle. He might be sitting by this river on the same day he had faced Ulfberht Longarm at dawn, a week later, or the week before. The only certainty was that he was governed by the pull of an object from that time. Before, it had been the amber. Now .... He returned his gaze to the chalice, bright and undented, in the centre of what remained of the picnic. It was undamaged as yet by its journey down the stream. 'Ulfberht Longarm plans to lay siege to Kilcarrigan Abbey,' he said, speaking with all the foreknowledge a twentieth-century history lesson could give. 'If you want to get your own back on the Lochlannachs, that's where you'll find some.'

His words had the effect of a handful of grain cast into a farmyard of chickens. There was a stir as all eyes were turned upon him. Pacifus, munching his way through his fifth meat pasty, was forgotten. 'I'll give them eggs!' said Maeve. 'I may not get my pig back, but one of his hams would come in useful,' Siobhan stated. 'There's room in my cellar for one or two more,' Fionnualla said grimly. 'To think of that Holy Place in barbarian hands!' Grania cried angrily. 'We must go at once.'

'I give the orders round here,' Queen Iseult reminded her coolly. 'But I agree. Girls! Pack up immediately. We're sailing on.'

The picnic was hastily stowed away and the washing-up done in record time. Earth was scattered on the fire to put out the flames. After a quick consultation, it was decided to sail up-stream. Grania, who had been to Kilcarrigan Abbey many times on pilgrimage, said that was the way to go. Once more, they took to the boat.

Away from the open sea the sail was useless. They were forced to row. After a while, the river became too narrow for the ship's long oars, and they had to tow it from the bank, using a rope made from the remaining fishing lines and belts from the women's abandoned dresses. However, Queen Iseult organised a rota, and when her turn came everyone pulled with a will. It seemed to Paul, heaving on the rope, no time at all before the slopes of the Knocknafeeny Mountains rose into view. He glanced at the sky. Not long after noon. 'Kilcarrigan Abbey!' Pacifus murmured happily beside him (he was not being much help with the pulling). 'We'll soon be home.'

'We'll anchor here,' declared Queen Iseult, 'creep up on the Lochlannachs, and take them unawares.'

'We'll larrup them!' Fionnualla cried. 'Hurray!'

'With what?' demanded Maeve. 'Grania threw all the weapons overboard.'

There was a deathly hush. Everyone looked accusingly at the prim little lady in the skirt ('My mother-in-law!' Emer whispered to Paul. 'Typical. She would!'). 'They looked so untidy,' Grania defended herself, 'left any old how in the bottom of the boat. Dirty, too. The blood was crusted on them.'

'No excuse,' Iseult said severely. 'Now, we're weaponless.' They looked at each other helplessly.

'Why are we all standing here like a herd of sheep?' Fionnualla cried suddenly. 'We're getting as bad as the men. Remember your handicraft training, girls. What would the Good Sisters say? There are stones in the river. Ash trees beyond the bank. The boat is moored beside a good strong blackthorn. And look over there! A whole grove of yew trees .... What we don't have, we make!'

Paul and Pacifus watched amazed as ash staves were cut and fashioned into spears, yew boughs bent into bows and strung with fishing line (another use for it!). Blackthorn was made into knobbly cudgels; stones were dredged from the river and knapped into sharp points. Fionnualla found a box of fish hooks in the prow, heated them over a fire and beat them into arrowheads, while Emer collected reed stems for shafts. Grania, forgiven for her excess of tidiness, took everybody's rings and bangles, and sewed them on to strips of strong linen to make armour. 'I don't like parting with my jewelry,' sighed Emer. 'But for a good cause ....'

'You'll get it back,' Grania assured her. 'I've made a list, each item by its owner's name.' The pile of weapons became impressive. It was finished just in time ....

'Look up there!' quavered Pacifus, pointing with a trembling finger towards the Knocknafeeny Mountains.

Standing on the brow of the hill, the sunlight beating on his helmet and coat of mail – and upon the axe in his hand – was Ulfberht Longarm!

CHAPTER 15
THE OLD MEN OF THE MOUNTAIN

Michael's head continued to spin long after his body had ceased all motion. Hatless (he had lost his bowler on the way), he lay face down, expecting at any moment to feel the sharp blade of the Viking's axe, and to lose his head as well – 'I won't miss it,' he reflected, 'it isn't up to much.' It was only the fact that the stone he had landed against was becoming colder and harder by the minute, and his face was buried in a cushion of moss (making breathing difficult and causing a beetle, living there, to explore the inside of his nose), which made him stir at last.

Michael sat up, sneezing loudly. Disentangling his handkerchief from the piece of amber, he blew his nose to rid it of the beetle. It seemed to him that the sudden noise caused the stone at his back to shudder, but he was shivering so hard himself he could not be certain. Looking about, he found he had rolled into the middle of a large prehistoric stone circle.

'I don't like such places. They scare me,' Michael muttered to himself. 'Gran says they're best to be avoided. She says the stones are hard.' Having felt this for himself, Michael rose stiffly to his feet. He had barely taken three steps when the moon, which had been behind a big black cloud, reappeared, flooding the hillside with light. Lifting his foot to take a fourth step, he became aware of eyes watching him.

Hair prickling at the back of his neck, Michael lowered his foot. Greatly daring, he turned around.

Silhouetted against the moonlit sky, the ancient limestone blocks loomed out of the heather like a giant set of broken teeth. If he should move, Michael felt, the great jaw would snap shut, and the earth swallow him. Scarcely allowing himself to breathe, he eyed the single stone in the centre of the circle ....

In its turn, the stone eyed him!

It took Michael's slow, fear-frozen brain some while to come to terms with what he was seeing. The longer he stood there, the more time he had to study the stone. Unlike those in the circle it had a head. Carved grooves suggested hair twisted into plaits on either side of a long thin face. The face was dominated by a pair of enormous eyes, staring at Michael balefully, and by a gaping mouth, through which the wind whistled as if the statue was sucking in each breath, only to spit it out again as useless. Since Michael was holding his own breath, almost to bursting, it was the only sound to be heard within the silence of the circle.

The best thing to be done, Michael decided, was to creep away while the statue was not looking. This proved to be impossible, so he had to choose the second best thing. Keeping his eyes upon it, and breathing as quietly as he could (unable to hold his breath any longer), he began to inch his way, step by step, round to the back of the statue where it could not see him. Having achieved his goal, he stopped appalled.

It is one thing to have eyes in the back of one's head (Gran, he always suspected, owned such a pair), quite another to have a whole face! Where at most he had expected to see the rest of the statue's strange hair-do, and the nape of its neck, there was a second identical,

long, thin face, open-mouthed ... and a pair of large eyes, watching him.

Michael stood on his blistered feet in the heather, and for a while the few wits he had deserted him. Perhaps it might have been merciful if the stone teeth of the circle had indeed closed, and the earth had swallowed him. It did not. When at last his wits returned, creeping back into his fuzzy head as timidly as mice, the statue was still there – still staring at him without a crack of difference in the expression on its face. Michael had every reason to suppose that the face on the other side gazed out across the heather, equally unchanged.

There was one thing about the statue that was different, though. Michael listened carefully. He could be wrong, but it seemed to him that the sound coming from its mouth had altered. No longer was it merely breathing (or, scornfully rejecting breath). Unless he was mistaken, he could hear words. The statue was whispering!

'What?' enquired the first face (the one on the far side, which could not see him).

'Who!' corrected its companion. The icy blast of the word hit Michael and made him shiver.

'Which?'

'Why?' meditated Face Number Two.

'Where?' demanded the face which had spoken first. There was an impatience in its voice which suggested to Michael that, if it could, it would have spun round like a weathercock and taken its turn in glaring at the intruder. 'Here!' hissed its companion equally aggressively. After this came a long silence, broken only by the whiffling of the wind through the heather beyond the stone edge of the circle. Both faces stared out blankly, apparently lost in contemplation.

'What?' began the first face at last (Michael could not be sure, but he thought something in the wind added 'is it?').

'One – of – Them.'

'Them?'

'Those!'

'Ahh!' (this from both statues)

'One of the "Quick Ones" ... passing through.'

'Through?'

'Over!' – 'By!' – 'Here' – 'There!' – 'Near' – 'Far!' – 'Away!' –'Fast!' – 'Too fast!' – 'Much too fast!!'

If a stone could become agitated, this stone was. Michael's eyes might have been deceiving him, but he swore he saw the stone quiver, then begin to shake. It started to rock so violently he feared it would come crashing down, squashing him like a tomato in the heather. Taking a hint from the word 'fast', he turned ... and fled.

'Wait!!'

There was no disobeying the order! Michael stood rooted to the spot. 'Come!' – 'Here!' Obedient as a well-trained dog, he turned and did as he was told.

Another lengthy pause. A new sound broke the silence of the circle: the sound of Michael's teeth chattering in his head. The statue continued to stare at him blankly. Michael was just beginning to wonder if, although its eyes were on him, its mind – if it had one – was not, and this was the moment to make his escape, when the face looking at him spoke once more.

'Man!' it said. The word was not uttered in a whisper. Rather, it came grating through the stone as if dredged up from the earth beneath. 'Man?' queried the other, after taking time to digest the news. 'Man,' confirmed its companion. There was a chilly hatred in its tones.

Having been identified for what he was, Michael felt he had been stared at enough. There was a new coldness seeping from the stone, creeping across the ground towards him. If he stayed any longer, he thought, he might become like it; there would be two stone figures standing in the heather. 'I don't want to spend the rest of Eternity looking at him,' he muttered. 'I haven't even got a face to look the other way.' The coldness carried a feeling of contempt. Contempt for what? His comparative smallness? Weakness? The softness of his flesh? The brittleness of his bones? Envy, too! Envy, perhaps, that he did not have to stand rooted forever where he had been placed. He was free to go. 'That's just what I'm going to do,' he told it. 'I'm not staying to look at your ugly mug. I'm off. And you can't stop me. You can't follow me, neither.' Without more ado, he leapt sideways – a big leap, which took him to the side of the statue where there was no face watching him. Away from the power of the big stone eyes, he was able to stumble to the circle's edge ....

He could go no further. One step over the rim, and the piece of amber in his pocket had him twisted up in agony.... Ulfberht Longarm was standing a mere three paces off, fingering his axe, and sneering at him.

Michael backed hastily behind the nearest limestone block. Breathing hard, he flattened himself against it. After a while, when the silence got too intense, he dared to peep round to find out what was happening. Ulfberht Longarm was still there; still fingering his axe. But there was a dark frown upon his face. His foot kept moving as if he wanted to step forward, but was unable. Met by something older and more stoney-hearted than himself and without the protection of his magic charm he did not dare to pass into the circle.

'Well! Here's a fine state of things,' said Michael to himself. 'I'm trapped. Stuck like a moth in a lighted window, between the cold wind and the flame.'

The thought was not attractive. Against his grandmother's warning Michael might have faced the Old Men of the Mountain, but he had come out of the experience with his brain surprisingly unharmed. He began to apply all the thinking power he had.

'There's one fella,' he said, gripping his right thumb with his left hand, 'that makes you feel so cold your brains freeze up like ice. And there's another,' (transferring the grip to his index finger) 'burns the leg off you whenever you go near him. Now, what one needs is a bit of heat. And the other needs cooling down a bit. How can I do that, I wonder?' He scratched his head. It was then he remembered the piece of amber (the cause of the pain in his leg, though he had not yet made the connection!). 'It carries the power of the sun,' his grandmother had said. 'So it does!' A smile broke out on Michael's moon-shaped face. 'When the sun's not out,' he told himself happily, 'you feel the cold. When it's there, you warm up nicely ... I'll give it a try.'

Sure enough, the closer he came to the centre of the circle the greater was the ease in the burning feeling in his leg. Looking back, Michael could still see the glint of the Viking's armour beyond the stones, but it seemed to him that the glow upon the bronze was growing fainter, as if Ulfberht Longarm was starting to fade away. On the other hand, the cold presence of the statue was still there sending a chill into his bones. Michael faced it. Bravely, he tried to outstare the eyes. With fingers numbed by ice he fumbled in his pocket, and took out the amber.

It was still warm, sending little darts of heat into his joints, and making movement easier. The new life in his fingertips gave Michael courage and determination. Without taking his eyes off the stony glare of his opponent, he knelt down, and holding the amber firmly in his left hand, dug a small hole at the base of the statue with his right. He dropped the piece of amber into the hole just where the feet of the statue should have been, if it had any. 'Gran always says if you warm your toes, you warm your heart as well,' he told it. Well aware that every moment might be watched by Ulfberht Longarm, he covered the hole, replaced the turf, and stamped it down firmly. Not even bothering to check if the expression on the face above had changed, he turned, and with his own heart a good deal lighter, marched purposefully towards the edge of the circle.

The Viking was not there. Michael passed between the stones with ease. As he reached the track which led downhill he heard a strange sound, coming from behind him. Half wail – half whistle – it seemed to rise into the moonlit sky, curling round the clouds, and falling to the earth once more. 'There now! His feet are warm, he's singing,' Michael said to himself with satisfaction. He was reminded of an old saying his grandmother was particularly fond of – one she used whenever a task was impossibly hard, or whenever Michael complained that something he wanted very much would never happen.

'*When Stones sing the Times will come together*,' he said aloud. Adding, his face splitting into a broad grin, 'That was a good job done!' His feet hit the road at the very spot where they had left it. As they did so, the moon paled and a bright light in the east showed that the long night was coming to an end at last. Whistling merrily, Michael turned for home.

He arrived to find Rosy had beaten him to it. Still in her shafts, she was standing in the yard. She was in an odd mood – uneasy, and fidgety – and refused to let him take off her harness.

Chapter 16
The Battle Of The Spotted Pig

Thirty-six faces turned towards the Knocknafeeny Mountains. Thirty-six pairs of eyes anxiously studied the Viking chief.

Ulfberht Longarm seemed unaware of the pirates' presence. He had his back to them, and was absorbed by something further up the hill. 'W-what do we do, now?' quavered Emer. She spoke in a whisper, despite the fact that Ulfberht was far enough away not to hear.

'I might be able to pick him off,' offered Fionnualla, gripping her longbow, and gauging the distance with one eye closed. 'He's just within my range. Standing there upon the hill he'd be an easy target.'

'In that coat of mail!' Iseult was scornful. 'The arrow would only bounce off, and you'd draw his attention to us.'

'Perhaps – we could surround him while he isn't looking,' Maeve suggested without much conviction. Nobody thought it a good idea. 'I think we should hide,' Pacifus said positively.

'I think we're wasting time,' Paul stated. 'We should proceed to the abbey while his back is turned and take his followers by surprise.' (The feel of a good strong blackthorn cudgel in his hand was giving him courage.) 'Too late for surprises,' cried Grania, the only one with the presence of mind to watch the river path. 'Someone's coming!'

Whoever it was, they were in a great hurry. Feet! Many of them – definitely an army! – pounded the path, causing the bank to shake. Shouts were heard. War-cries, surely? The air was split by a fiendish racket – 'Haw-hee-haw ...!' Round the corner, long ears laid back, burst Rosy, at a gallop, drawing the bouncing, swaying donkey cart behind. Inside, Michael – looking shaken – was clinging for dear life. 'Whoah!' cried Paul, jumping to catch the flapping reins. Rosy shied, and skidded. The cart tipped over and, Michael All-alone landed with a bump at their feet.

'What's happening to me, now?' he asked feebly, as Paul put out a hand to help him up. 'Where am I at all? As if stones that speak and fellas with sharp axes are not enough! Who are these?' He gazed fearfully at the circle of strange faces. 'They're friends,' Paul hastily assured him. 'Friendly pirates,' he added rather grandly, 'come to help us to fight the Vikings.'

'Is that so?' Michael did not sound convinced. He rubbed his chin (he was in need of a shave, for there had been little time that morning for anything other than a quick splash of face and hands in the water butt). 'Odd!' he murmured. 'But then everything is odd today. Look at the river, now. It's further up the bank than usual. The path looks different. And the hills. There's too many trees about. It's as if I've come to a new country, altogether.'

'Not new,' Paul corrected him (he was becoming quite experienced in these matters!). 'More old, really.' Michael, deep in his own worries, was not listening to him.

'Yes, odd!' he said. 'And I'm not one for oddness. I leave that to Gran. Here am I without a wink of sleep, having been dragged up mountains, and forced to talk to stones. I come home to find the hens hismissterrical with starvation, their eggs all scrambled, the cock is crowing fit to split his wings, and the ducks are threatening to drown themselves. To make matters worse, Tantony has given up hope of breakfast altogether, and has gone off rootling on his own. When I take the donkey cart to go and look for him, Rosy acts as if she's got prickles in her harness and goes at a pace she's never tried before. Just as I'm getting to the place where I think Tantony might be, you jump out in front of me, and everything changes .... For the worse, if you ask me. Now you tell me I've got to go and fight the Vikings. With those!' He indicated the ladies with a lack of gallantry that would not have pleased his Gran.

'Now, look here! I'm as good as any man. Better!' Fionnualla loomed in front of him, waving her bow and arrow. Things might have turned nasty for Michael. But, at that moment, all attention was switched to the Knocknafeeny Mountains.

There came a squeal that could have wakened every stone upon the hill, whether it had a face or not. Tantony came hurtling into view, bouncing and rolling like a pink and black football down the hill. Ulfberht Longarm sprang to life. Like the needle on a compass, he whirled around. His glittering hand-axe cut a swathe in the sky before landing with a thud within inches of the pig's flying trotters. Tantony squealed even louder, arriving in a state of collapse on the far side of the river.

'Don't be trying to cross, you know you can't swim.' Michael plunged into the water to rescue his pet. 'All hands to the pig!' ordered Queen Iseult. Together, they dragged the struggling, dripping animal onto the bank. He rolled over, and closed his eyes. 'Don't die on me, I'd miss you sorely.' Michael fell to his knees beside him. 'Gracious, goodness!' he cried, 'what's this, he's holding in his mouth?'

'It's the amber!' Paul realised. 'I don't know how he's done it, but his rootling has managed to turn up Thor's Hammer. Quick! We must get it away from him before the Viking arrives.'

'Drop!' 'Give!' 'Leave it!' 'Let – go!' They tried every command they knew. Tantony – eyes still closed – merely clenched his teeth the tighter, and refused to give up his prize. 'He'll be here at any minute!' despaired Maeve, glancing over her shoulder at the fast approaching Viking.

'Wait! I have an idea. There's one honey cake left.' Emer dashed to fetch it.

On her return Tantony opened one piggy eye, and fixed it upon the honey cake. He lifted his snout, and the tip of his nose began to quiver. 'Good boy,' encouraged Emer, waving the cake tantalisingly beyond his reach. The pig grinned up at her. Grunting, he began to heave himself to his feet. There came a snap – a gulp! The honey cake disappeared. So did the piece of amber!

'Look what you've done! He's after swallowing it.' Michael was frantic.

'I don't think amber will do him any harm. Pigs have a strong digestion,' Paul tried to comfort him. 'All the same,' he added, 'I think we should get him away from here before Ulfberht crosses the river. With that sharp axe he might slice him into rashers, looking for his charm.'

With a great deal of difficulty, and much pushing and heaving, they managed to get the pig aboard the donkey cart. Rosy, oblivious of the drama played out

around her, was contentedly nibbling white flowers from the blackthorn bush. 'Giddup!' cried Michael, yanking her head around. 'We're going home. If we can find it amongst all these trees.' He cracked his whip. 'Now,' Paul said grimly, turning to the ladies, 'some delaying tactics, to help them get away. Any ideas?'

There followed what Paul, writing in his diary later, was to call 'The Battle of the Spotted Pig.' It was fought between the Vikings and the pirates on the broad meadow, beneath the orchard, with the grey walls of Kilcarrigan Abbey looking down upon the combatants. For the whole afternoon, the battle raged the struggling foe locked in close combat slashing at each other as they pressed this way and that before the abbey walls. Soon the long flowering grass of the meadow was flattened, and stained with blood, and the apple trees began to bear the scars of sword thrusts and axe-blows which had gone astray. It seemed at first that victory might go to either side, for the pirates fought bravely, and the Vikings seemed lacking in heart. Rumour had it that their chief was refusing to take part; he had lost his sword and was sulking in the quarry. 'Soon flush him out,' boasted Fionnualla .... 'Come out of that, ya little rat, ya!' When she looked, he wasn't there.

Towards evening, the Vikings' superior experience and strength began to tell, and rumours flew once more. Reports came in that Ulfberht had found his sword at last, and had joined the battle. Dreadful bloody deeds occurred – now in this place, now in that part of the melee. But nobody caught sight of him. 'They're cheating, that's what it is,' grumbled Iseult, ducking and dodging to avoid the bombardment of a burly fellow with one eye. 'That method of attack was never in the Rules of Combat.'

'What are your friends in the abbey doing in all this?' panted Paul to Pacifus, as he fended off the blows of a huge bearded bully, armed to the teeth with evil-looking knife, battle-axe and spiked cudgel. 'We're fighting to save their skins. Surely they could come out for a while, and help?'

'They're men of peace, like me,' the monk said primly. 'Take that, you hairy divil!' He smashed the Viking's helmet round his ears. He appeared to be enjoying himself.

Slowly, gradually, the pirates were tiring. Slowly, gradually, they were being pushed back towards their boat. Had it not been for the timely, and – judging from the look on his face – unexpected return of Michael All-alone, armed with his old shotgun and a pocketful of bird pellets, they would have been soundly beaten. What Queen Iseult had ordered as a dignified retreat would have become a disorderly rout.

'Don't know what I'm doing back here, again,' he said grimly. 'When I thought I was safely settled in my own place. I only wanted a few rooks for the pot. Still, while I'm about it ....' Sounding off, he peppered Vikings right and left. Under cover of his fire, Iseult was able to withdraw her followers to a small knoll where, sheltered by a ruined rath, Grania had set up her field hospital for the wounded of both sides ('Fairness in everything, I always say,' she stated firmly, 'Besides,' she added astutely, 'there's bound to be an advantage in having them as hostage.'). Here, they held a Council of War.

'I vote we go on fighting.' Fionnualla had suffered a black eye, a bump on the head, and she had one arm in a sling. But she swore these were minor injuries.

'We're all exhausted,' protested Maeve, 'and Siobhan, here, is badly hurt. We need a rest.' There were murmurs of agreement.

'What we must do,' Queen Iseult stated firmly, 'is take the opportunity of a lull in the battle' (having never met birdshot before, the Vikings had all dived into the quarry) 'to study our objectives. Now, what was Objective Number One?'

'To save Tantony from Ulfberht Longarm,' replied Paul, 'and, although we still don't know where Ulfberht is, Michael assures me Tantony is safely tucked into his sty.'

'So, Objective Number One has been achieved,' said Iseult. 'I think everyone here will agree it was worth the sacrifice.' Agreement was muted. Siobhan, who was unconscious, said nothing at all.

'That's that, then. We can end this silly pantomime.' Grania began to roll up her bandages. 'About time too, I'd say.'

'Wait! Not so fast.' Iseult glared at her. 'You're forgetting Objective Number Two.'

All eyes were turned on Paul. Miserably, he cleared his throat. 'Objective Number Two was to get Pacifus and his chalice to the abbey, I suppose,' he said reluctantly. 'Can't we forget it? I mean, with all those bullies in the way I don't see how we can. At the rate he's going Michael will soon run out of bird shot.' (How he wished he could get the witch's words – 'Your promise!' – out of his head!)

War weariness settled on them all. Even Fionnualla was silent. Nobody was prepared to make a suggestion. Grania prescribed a tonic. But when she looked she found the bottle empty. 'What we could do with is your Gran, and her advice,' Paul said to Michael sourly (he just could not get her nagging from his mind).

'Gran's not here.' Michael stated the obvious. 'But I know what she would say.' Sending a final volley in the direction of the quarry, he put down his gun .... 'When stones sing, the Times will come together,' he pronounced, flushed with his success and proud to have remembered the lesson.

Everyone looked blank .... But Michael suddenly became very excited.

'Begob! I see what she means!' he cried, capering about.

'Oh, do stop jigging and sit down,' growled Fionnualla. 'Your dancing hurts my head.' 'Besides, you're drawing attention to us,' added Iseult (Michael's whoops of joy were giving rise to furious cat-calls from the quarry).

Michael would not be put off. He did not get many ideas, and when one came into his head it stayed there. 'Look-it, don't you see?' he insisted, almost bursting with pride and agitation. 'They were singing happily enough when I left them, but of course thanks to Tantony's rootling the heat is gone. His feet are cold again. So they've fallen quiet.'

'What on earth are you talking about?' Paul demanded.

'That's just it. The earth! The earth where his feet should be has gone cold.'

'Who's feet?' Plainly the battle had gone to Michael's head!

'The big stone on the hill,' he was shouting. 'The one with two faces. If Ulfberht Longarm himself was scared of it – and him all covered in mail, and that –

doesn't it stand to reason the other Vikings will be frightened, too? They just need the stone brought to their notice. All we need is a good bit of heat to warm his toes and he'll sing again. Really loud ...! I don't know about it making the Times come together, but if it frightens the Vikings maybe they'll run away, leaving the field clear. I can make a big bonfire out of dried heather .... Has anybody got a light?'

'There's my tinder-box,' Grania said doubtfully. 'But I don't usually lend ....'

'That'll do.' Michael snatched the precious object from her hand. 'You have that little fella and his chalice ready to go to the abbey when I give the signal,' he said to Paul. 'I won't be long.'

'What is the signal?' Paul began. Michael All-alone was no longer there.

'Well, really! I always knew he was a bit soft in the head, but ...' Paul turned to speak to Pacifus. 'Where is he?' Paul cried wildly. 'He was here only a minute ago.'

'While you were all busy nattering,' Grania was at her most self-righteous, 'some of us had jobs to do. Brother Pacifus has been very useful. He was helping me to tend the wounded. His knowledge of herbal remedies has been invaluable. When he mentioned a herb growing by the river I ....'

'The river?' Time spun in Paul's head .... 'Round and round!' Michael's Gran had said. 'Like the tracks on a toy railway .... Till somebody changes the points!' *That* was what Michael was about to do! All at once, Paul knew what the consequences of Michael's bonfire would be. *When stones sing the Times will come together*. In all innocence, Michael was about to make Past and Present meet, cross, and part forever into the future .... And Pacifus! Pacifus was down by the river

... where it all began. 'No!' he screamed. 'No!!' His only answer was mocking laughter from the quarry. The Vikings – now that Michael had ceased shooting – were starting to crawl from their hiding-place, to attack once more. 'If you have any arrows left,' he said to Emer, standing next to him, 'shoot them, now, while I make a dash for it. I have to save Pacifus before it is too late.'

Vaulting over the crumbling defences, he set off at a run.

CHAPTER 17
WHEN STONES SING

Shouts rose from the Vikings. They had spotted him!
Paul felt the ground vibrate as three of them gave
chase. He heard the whine of an arrow through the
air and the crash of a heavy body hitting the ground.
'Well done, Emer!' he had time to think, but did not
dare to slow his pace.

The second Viking stumbled over the body of his
friend; Paul heard him swear. He could tell from the
sounds that the third man was drawing nearer and
would soon catch him up. 'I'll have to turn and fight,'
he thought, steeling himself. Then he realised he was
unarmed. In his hurry, he had neglected to pick up
his blackthorn cudgel.

Thinking on his feet, Paul swerved and made a
dash for the cover of the forest. It would take him
longer to go that way, with no path through the dense
undergrowth. Still, a young agile boy might have
more chance of escaping the large clumsy men
following him. If the worst came to the worst, he
could always hide. In the event, this was what he was
forced to do, for in no time at all he had run up against
a thicket of brambles. Fortunately, there was a large
beech with boughs bending almost to the ground
growing nearby. He had just time to grab a branch
and swing himself up when a splintering of wood,
and the shaking of the foliage down below, warned
him the Vikings were using their axes to cut a way

through. Presently, the rounded domes of two Viking helmets came into view.

On reaching the tree the men stopped. Tucking himself into an angle where the branch met the trunk, Paul prayed they would not look up. From where he crouched he could hear their voices, but was not able to understand what they were saying, for they spoke in Norse. If only, he thought, they would move on! Instead, they started to thrash about with their axes, slashing the brambles, searching for him. Paul felt his legs growing leaden with cramp; and knew he was about to fall. Reaching out for something to save himself, his hand met a dead stick. It cracked, gave way, and landed right on top of a stooping Viking. Grunting, the man straightened his back. He was in the very act of looking up, when his companion shouted something and pointed.

An animal was charging towards them through the forest. Paul was able to mark its progress by the frenzied movement of the bushes like a tidal wave. He could hear its snorting breath. Its snorts reminded him of Tantony. But never had he seen such a pig as burst upon them. Lean and black and hairy, it had yellowish tusks protruding from its slavering mouth, and tiny eyes, red with fury. It brought with it a stench that was almost overwhelming. Crashing to a halt, it stood, rib-cage heaving, as it tested the air with its long mobile snout. Locating the intruders on its territory, it gave a scream of rage, and charged .... Like all men of their time, the Vikings knew better than to face a wild boar in a temper. Leaping through the brambles and dodging in and out amongst the trees, they fled.

Paul waited long enough to allow the sounds of the chase to fade into the distance. Then he slithered from the tree. He had to draw back to allow the wild boar's mate and her brood of squealing, pyjama-striped piglets to pass by (luckily he was downwind of them and the sow, short-sighted like all those of her kind, did not notice him). He made his way with all possible speed out of the forest. Better to face capture – even death – at the hands of the Vikings, he decided, than the unknown terror of wild beasts.

When he emerged, it was to find that the Vikings and the pirates were joined in battle once again. He was able to slip on unnoticed. Creeping along the margin of the forest, he made for the river bank. The glint of water was in sight, and he had begun with relief to quicken his pace, when the strange 'music' reached his ears.

Paul stood stock-still. He listened while prickles ran up and down his spine, like the fingers of a concert pianist. So this was what stones sounded like when they sang! Michael's bonfire had been successful; the cries of the warriors and the clanging of their weapons were drowned by a keening from the hills. Soon, as the singing of the stones rose and fell, the noise of the battle began to slide away. If he was not quick, Paul realised, he would be too late to save Pacifus from whatever fate awaited him when the Times changed. He had to reach the river before the singing stopped! A few steps further on something caught his attention, bringing him once more to a halt.

At the edge of the forest there stood a beehive hut, woven of branches. As far as he could tell it was deserted. Beside the hut grew a sapling tree, a rowan. He could see its creamy flower bracts and its fingered leaves. Thrust into the mossy ground beneath the tree was a sword.

Paul crept forward. It was Ulfberht Longarm's sword. He recognised the pair of dragons writhing on the blade, the semi-precious stones clustered round an empty gap which should have held a charm. Nervously, he eyed the small dark entrance to the hut. ... Was he being lured into a trap? Was the Viking, even now, watching him with his hard, sapphire eyes? As he hesitated the weird singing began to fade. A breeze sprang up, rustling the sapling's leaves.

All at once, Paul's mind was taken back ... forward? Over? (Did it matter?) There was another small house. Of stone. With smoke rising crookedly from its chimney. Leaves, rustled by the breeze. An ancient rowan (surely not as old as eleven hundred years?). Singing, too! The musical purring of the witch's cats. Her own strange, wordless song .... 'Until you need the sword,' she had said – 'I won't need it,' he had thought. 'It isn't mine.' ... He was weaponless. Beside the river (he knew it, now) stood a fearsome foe, the sword's owner. Waiting to be overcome.

A few tattered echoes of the music still reverberated round the hills. There would never be another chance! Paul sprang towards the sword. Seizing its hilt, he pulled it from the ground. Without a backward glance towards the hut, heedless of the weight of the weapon in his hands, he raced towards the river bank .... What his eyes met there was so familiar he imagined he must have witnessed it many times before.

'Round and round! The circle was complete!' The river murmured sleepily across the stones. Somewhere, hidden, a blackbird was singing its heart out in the middle of a bush. The late afternoon sun was casting spangles on the ripples of the water, and flashing upon the sides of a magnificent jewelled cup.

Caught in a whirlpool, the Kilcarrigan Chalice was spinning. Round and round!

Two men were at the water's edge. The first, a plump young man with a shaved tonsure, and a coarse brown habit tucked above his knees, was struggling desperately to tear a branch from a nearby blackthorn tree. In doing so, he was making a considerable noise. But the other man ignored him. Nor did he seem to see Paul. Tall, and lean, and scar-faced – his long blonde hair tumbling beneath his winged helmet, brushing the shoulders of his glinting coat of mail – he stood transfixed. His eyes were upon the chalice, twirling in the water.

It was all about to happen again – that fatal fight for the possession of the cup! But, Paul had Ulfberht Longarm's sword. He gripped it tightly in both hands. Taking a deep breath, he judged the spot he would have to reach, where the Viking's sun-reddened neck rose above his shirt and coat of mail (almost, he thought, he could see the pulse of life throbbing beneath the skin!). He raised the heavy sword as high as he was able ... and lunged ....

What went wrong he never knew. Certainly, as he realised afterwards, a small boy had little chance of wounding so tall and strong and practised a warrior. Eyes tight shut against the enormity of what he was about to do, Paul heard the sword tip clang as it meet the coat of mail, and jets of pain went shooting up his arm. A blow from nowhere caught him on the side of the head and sent him reeling. He was plunged into a blackness, thick as tar, and sank slowly through the choking dark to what felt like the very centre of the earth. Taking a thousand years to reach it .... Until .... From somewhere far away came a voice whispering at his ear. 'Just where do you think you're going?

hissed Michael's Gran. A hand – small and birdlike –
grabbed him by the collar, pulling him upwards.
Supported by the hand, Paul began to struggle.
Dog-paddling with what remained of consciousness,
back to the surface. When, finally, the hand let go, and
sight returned, he was lying flat on his back, still by
the river. Ulfberht Longarm was looming over him ...
Sword in hand!

Paul knew then how an animal must feel, when
faced with its end at the hands of a butcher. Utterly
helpless, he sprawled upon the ground. He tried to
speak, pleading for his life. But no words came. If
they had, doubtless Ulfberht would have neither
understood, nor cared. With a glint of steel in his hard,
blue eyes he braced himself on his booted feet, and
raised his sword.

'For – the – abbey!!'

Something small and brown had burst between them. With a flurry of coarsely woven cloth, it sprang – catching Ulfberht's sword arm, and clinging to it. A pair of sandalled feet went swinging high above the ground.

Caught, poised to strike, the Viking chief was overbalanced. There came a crash, the clang of heavy metal as it hit a stone. A brief struggle. A splash ... And all was still.

'Pacifus?'

Shakily, Paul rose to his feet. His glasses were lopsided on his nose and the world was spinning, faster than the chalice. With trembling hands he tried to straighten them. He was unaware he had reached the river's brink until he felt cold water seeping through his shoes. Stupidly, he stared at it and wondered why it was stained red.

Ulfberht Longarm's body was floating in the shallows, with scarlet waves fanning round where his sword was lodged firmly in his throat. Nearby, half out of the water, lay something that looked like a bundle of old sacks.

'Pacifus!'

As gently as he could Paul pulled his friend onto the bank, and turned him over. 'He'll get up,' he kept assuring himself. 'He did the last time. When it happened before ... He was all right, then ....'

There was a small scarlet circle – about the size of a bullseye on a dart board – glistening beyond a rip in Pacifus's habit, somewhere in the region of his heart. Hastily Paul pulled out his handkerchief, and tried to stem the flow of blood.

Pacifus's eyelids fluttered. He opened his eyes. When he saw Paul bending over him he grinned, and the twinkle in his eye was almost mischievous.

'I – didn't step aside this time, did I?' he said proudly. 'So I'm not a coward after all. Maybe, some day, they'll even say that I'm a martyr.'

'No!' Paul wanted to shout. 'You can't be a martyr, I won't let you. You're a ghost already so how can you die twice?'

But he could tell from the stillness gathering on the river bank that he was too late. Already, the music from the hills had ceased. Time was changing. Murmuring something about 'angels', Pacifus closed his eyes. He was beginning to fade, and could not hear him. Looking up, Paul saw the chalice, still spinning like a planet on the eddy. Gradually, the vision blurred. He could hear a choking sound coming from his throat. He knew that he was crying.

CHAPTER 18
THE TIMES COME TOGETHER

'Miaow! Miaow!'

The sound wove its way persistently amongst his sobs. Paul caught his breath, and managed to stop crying. Grabbing off his glasses, he rammed his fists, infantlike, into his eyes, as if he would smash the tears. Giving the lenses a quick wipe he replaced them on his nose, and glared at the intruder on his grief. 'How did you get here?' he demanded.

The witch's ginger cat glared back, without so much as a gleam of sympathy in its unblinking eyes. Glancing over its arching back Paul saw the answer to his question. The witch herself was poised upon the bank, trying to catch the chalice in her grandson's landing net. After the third attempt she pulled it to the shore, and brought it to him. 'A job is not well done until you've finished it,' she remarked, severely, dumping it at his feet.

Paul picked up the Kilcarrigan Chalice. It had been stolen, passed from one hand to another, whisked across the miles and over the centuries, sent floating down the river ... even used as the feeding-bowl for a pig! It appeared surprisingly undamaged. Of course, there was still the dent the restorers had not managed to remove; and a piece of blue enamel was still missing from its rim. The 'Tiger's Eyes' stared up at him, unblinking like the cat's. He drew his gaze away, turning to the grassy bank where his friend had been lying; the river, flowing pure and clear across the

164

stones. Both empty! There was not so much as a flattening of the grass. It was as if the struggle had not happened – as if the monk and his mortal enemy had never been.

'I've failed, haven't I?' he said wretchedly.

'What do you mean, failed?' The witch's eyes flashed at the very idea. 'As I said, a job is not well done until you've finished it. How can you be sure it is ever finished? What do you plan to do next?'

'Take this back to Grandfather, I suppose.' Paul's answer was sulky. He wished the witch would stop bullying him, and leave him alone. He wanted nothing so much as a good, long sleep ... and one of Mrs. McQuaid's large meals (it felt like centuries since he had eaten). The witch, however, had no intention of leaving him alone. Grabbing him in a clutch like a bird's, she heaved him to his feet and propelled him before her along the river path. Tail carried in the manner of a standard bearer, the ginger cat led the way.

They reached the spot where Queen Iseult had anchored the pirate ship. Was it only hours, or eleven hundred years ago? Paul, stumbling with exhaustion, could not quite remember. Mr. McQuaid's Friesian cows were grazing in the fields where the battle had been raging, peacefully swishing their lean piebald flanks with their long, supple tails. The only warlike sound was the pop-popping of Michael's gun beyond the sycamores, where he was shooting into the air to frighten the rooks. Paul would have liked to linger by the disused quarry (abandoned now by the archaeologists, for Grandfather had been told in Dublin that the money available for his excavations had run out). He wanted to recall his own brave deeds, see once again the flash of sunlight on dangerous weapons, and hear Queen Iseult's calm voice giving orders. Perhaps, he thought, if he stood very still, he might see Emer, shaking her dark curls beneath her helmet and laughing at him; or Fionnualla with her strong hands fitting an arrow to a bow; Grania, tut-tutting with disapproval as she guided a wounded warrior to a place of safety .... Michael's Gran would hear of no such sentimentality. Rubber boots working with a purpose, her many-coloured rags ruffled like a goldfinch's plumage, she marched him up the slope towards the abbey ruins.

Here, she abandoned him, sending him forward among the scattered stones with a shove. 'Come, Thomas!' she called over her shoulder to the ginger cat. 'It's suppertime. Your kittens are all waiting.' Turning, she stomped off in her old boots.

'Hold on,' Paul called after her. 'You haven't told me what you want me to do.'

'Me? Want?' The witch paused beneath the encircling sycamores. Michael had ceased his battle with the rooks and the inhabitants of the branches, triumphant, were guffawing at his defeat. It was hard to hear what she was saying, but even at that distance Paul could see her black eyes, challenging him. 'Why should I want anything? It has nothing to do with me. You made a promise. Remember? Come, Tom.' Reluctantly the cat left his investigation of a fieldmouse nest, and followed her.

His 'promise'! The ghosts might have vanished, but Paul, clutching the silver chalice, still felt haunted. Gloomily, he surveyed the abbey ruins. Little remained of the place Pacifus and his fellow monks had known. Half-shutting his eyes – and with Mr. O'Mahony's history lessons to supply the information – he tried to imagine it as it would have been.

The surrounding wall would have stood thick and tall. There would have been a stout wooden gate with bars set into it. Beyond would have lain that carefully tended mix of village, farm, and church that Pacifus called 'home'. Beehive huts, for the monks to sleep in, and larger buildings, providing shelter for travellers; kitchens, the refectory, the hospital with its garden of herbs. There would have been pens and byres to house the animals, and a grain store and its threshing-floor, a forge, a barn, a well. The brothers would have cultivated vegetables; they would have kept geese and ducks and pigs, doves in a dove-cote, honey bees in straw beehives set in niches in the walls ... In the centre – the hub of the wheel – stood the church, with its belltower and its carved cross beside it.

The great cross was gone, smashed by the Vikings (only a few fragments had been found). There was not much of the church left, either; just the low bare outline of the walls, and half the arch of the east window, crooked like a finger beckoning to the sky. Would that have been the altar? That stone slab lying in the nettles? Gingerly, Paul stepped through a gap which once had held the door ...

And, then it happened! Paul wondered at first why his eyesight was growing dim. Perhaps my glasses need cleaning again, he thought. He was aware of the rough grass beneath his feet, the cool evening breeze upon his face, the garrulous cawing of the rooks above his head, greeting each straggler, flying in from the fields to roost. From where he stood he was able to see Michael – gun tucked underneath his arm, barrel pointing for safety towards the ground –

walking away towards his cottage. To Paul's increasingly blurred sight his broad back seemed strangely fuzzy at the edges, as if viewed through the folds of a particularly thick net curtain. 'I must be tired,' he said to himself, recalling that he had not slept the night before (unless you counted being hit on the head by Fionnualla and knocked unconscious for a while). He switched his attention to some closer object. The crystals on the chalice leapt and swirled like the eddies on the river. He closed his eyes.

When he opened them again, he almost wished he hadn't. Time was spinning. Everything was moving at a dizzying speed. Trees – stones – the grass – the broken arch – were twirling by so fast they seemed to have become blended into one continuous whole; a swirling ribbon of changing colours with no break between. Now the colours were becoming mixed and confused, stirred to a single shade .... It was like watching the fairground from a whirling roundabout, the edge of the track (sleepers and posts and rails) from a racing Intercity train! 'Change the points.' 'The Times will come together.' 'When stones sing ...!'

Surely they were singing. He could hear them! Men's voices, raised in song. They were coming from the stones of the church which were rising higher and higher as they spun. The elm trees seemed to be closing in above his head. Fluttering figures of rooks were landing all around. Hugged tight to his chest, the chalice became the only solid object in a swirling melting pot of sound and vision; the only safe link through the centuries. Where was it taking him? Paul stumbled forward. If he could reach the centre of the chaos, he might find ....

Peace! ... Warm and sheltering, the walls rose up on either side to meet the stone corbals of the roof. Light poured through the tall, round-topped windows, forming golden pools on the smooth flags of the floor. Everywhere, there were candles; bright flames fluttering, like yellow bees sucking the wax with their flickering tongues, tinging the air with a scent of honey. Years of candle-smoke had turned the once white, limewashed walls to the colour of pale parchment, darkened the roof beams so that, looking up, they seemed to be melting into velvet night. As the singing of the monks faded, Paul could hear the furtive shuffling of their sandalled feet and knew that they were watching him from underneath their hoods. He stood quietly, scarcely daring to intrude. The chalice felt light as tinsel in his hands. Somewhere beyond this vision – this final glimpse – into the Past lay his own time, humdrum and ordinary, with its small achievements and disappointments, its happy moments and its sad ones – the 'Present' everyday world, to which he knew he must return. Go back to school; study his lessons; play with his friends. Grow up.

In the meantime, he was being allowed to fulfill his promise! Fixing his eyes upon the altar, with its crucifix, and the row of carved stone saints on either side, he began, step by step, to move down the church between the lines of waiting figures. Halfway, there came a disturbance in the quiet ranks. A frantic whispering could be heard. The sound of feet became something more than a discreet shuffle. Out of the corner of his eye, Paul noticed two of the brothers (one tall and lean, the other short – hardly bigger than himself – and rather stout) arguing fiercely. Fighting the thin hand crowned by sharp nails which tried to hold him back, the smaller man broke loose, and stepped out in front of Paul.

Paul's eyes met those of Pacifus. Round and blue; sparkling with mischief. Despite the solemnity of the occasion, he winked. 'Over to you, Brother!' he murmured haltingly in the old Irish language. He passed the Kilcarrigan Chalice to his friend.

'I've found it, Father! Didn't I tell you I would?' ... The sharp intake of breath registered Brother Gentilis's disapproval, but the kindly-looking man kneeling at the altar seemed unconcerned by the interruption to his prayers. Rising, he turned and smiled a welcome to the small dumpy figure making its way eagerly towards him. Reaching out, he received the chalice from Pacifus's hands. He held it high for all to see before placing it in its rightful spot upon the altar.

Once more, the monks' voices rose in song. Paul took one last look at the Kilcarrigan Chalice: there, on the high altar, with myriads of candle flames dancing on its silver surface. Reluctantly, he turned away .... 'Is that all right, Gran?' he asked the bright empty air above his head. With the vision fading all about him, he walked towards the door.

'Paul! Where have you been, lad? Mrs. McQuaid has been sick with worry. The gardai have been scouring the countryside.'

Grandfather was standing beyond the broken arch! Paul shook his head to rid his ears of the last of the singing voices (amazingly, the rooks were silent!). Taking off his glasses, he rubbed the candlelight from his eyes. 'Coming, Grandfather,' he called.

'Grandfather! You'll never guess ....' Careless of being stung, he doubled back, bursting through the bed of nettles to snatch the silver chalice from the slab of fallen stone.

'I've found the Kilcarrigan Chalice!' he announced, quite overlooking the grand speech he had prepared.

Some months later, there was an important exhibition at the National Museum in Dublin (everyone who considered themselves 'anyone' was there!). 'Treasures of a Lost Time', it was called. It featured, amongst others, the fine items discovered by Professor Sheean in and around the Kilcarrigan Abbey site. The Professor, himself, was a guest of honour at the opening reception. Hair sleeked down, shoes polished, in his best suit, Paul accompanied his grandfather.

The Kilcarrigan Chalice – its crystals glistening and its silver sides glinting beneath the light of many lamps – drew much comment and attention (everyone had read in the newspapers of its recent disappearance). An ancient Viking sword, with garnets and carnelians set into its hilt, caused much interest, too.

'Clever of Michael's Gran to find it in the river,' said Grandfather. 'She's a remarkable old woman. People say she's a witch, you know.' Taking out his eyeglass, he peered at the pattern on the blade. 'Came up well, the restorers did a good job,' he remarked to Paul. 'Just look at those dragons! Pity we never found the piece of amber. That rogue Vincent swears he doesn't know what happened to it. I don't believe him.'

Paul said nothing. Nor did he look too closely at the blade! The last time he had seen those dragons they had been just too near to him for comfort. He shivered. It was as well the sword was not complete, he thought. Add the amber charm, and one could not tell what might happen. 'Thor's Hammer' was safer where it was – tucked into the soft, rumbling folds of Tantony's stomach.

Once they had posed beside the chalice for Press photographs, Grandfather drew Paul aside. 'Come and take a look at these,' he said.

Ranged along one wall of the room, each upon its own plinth, stood a row of quaint, stone figures – 'Statues of Saints, 9th C., A.D., on loan from Museums in Brussels, Paris, and Rome,' the description card read. The statues were badly worn; some had no noses, others no chins, a few, indeed, had only half a face.

'Strange!' Grandfather paused beside a figure at the end of the row (better preserved than the rest). It represented a small, plump man in the habit of a monk – round-cheeked, with a head rather like an egg, big-eyed, a babyish expression. 'Look at this.' Puzzled, he placed his hands on his grandson's shoulders. 'The fellow I got to carve the copies for the church must have made a mistake. This statue is carrying something in his hands, the one in the church is empty-handed.'

Paul squinted back at his grandfather. He was finding it difficult not to laugh. 'Looks as if he's carrying the Kilcarrigan Chalice, don't you think?' he said.

'You're right!' Grandfather's beard jutted with pleasure. Behind their gold-rimmed spectacles, his hazel eyes were sparkling. 'Tell you what,' he said. 'Now that we've found the chalice again, I'll give that woodcarver fellow some new work to do. He can make a replica. We'll give it to the statue in the church.'

The room was crammed with a great many important people: gentlemen from the press, Dublin Officials, knowledgeable professors from many different lands, the Minister of Culture, who had opened the Exhibition. Conversation died. All eyes were turned towards Professor Sheean and his grandson, as Paul flung his arms about his grandfather and gave him a big hug. (Those in the know, of course, were not surprised, as they always said the two were odd!) 'Thank you,' he said. Adding something his grandfather did not quite understand:

'Pacifus will be pleased!'

The Sandclocker
Jack Scoltock

A historical adventure set at the time of the Spanish Armada, this is the story of two cousins, Diego and Tomas, who run away to sea to fight the English. Life on board the *Trinidad Valencera* is vividly described – scurvy, seasickness, lice and canon fire. The boys fear for their lives in storm after storm and raging sea battles. Gripping stuff written by one of the divers who discovered the Armada wreckage off the coast of Kinnago Bay in 1971.

ISBN 0 86327 531 1

Sea Wolves from the North
Michael Mullen

Sigmund the Red, a young Viking adventurer, leads his sea wolves southwards. On Iona, panic spreads – they must protect the priceless treasure they have spent years creating. Diarmuid, the boy monk, is charged with protecting the golden book. To save it, they must risk the dangers of Corrievrechan whirlpool. A sea chase full of suspense and excitement begins.

A brilliant book ... a good nail-biting adventure
E. Badrian (age 11) Books Ireland.

ISBN 0 86327 454 4

A Girl and a Dolphin
Patrick O'Sullivan

What would it be like to see a real wild dolphin? Anna
finds out when an unexpected visitor swims into her secret
cove – a bottle nosed dolphin! As the summer slips by,
their unusual friendship grows.

But the local fishermen don't want unwelcome guests in
their waters, and Donal's diving for sunken treasure must
remain undisturbed. In a story full of drama and
adventure, Patrick O'Sullivan captures all the magic of a
wild creature living close to humans.

Inspired by Fungi the Dingle dolphin

ISBN 0 86327 426 9

A Right Royal Pain
Aislinn O'Loughlin

Rumpelstiltskin: The True Story
When Rummy's best friend Shakademus (the Blackbird
with the BIG voice), tells him that the miller's daughter is
in trouble, Rummy decides to help her out. He expects to
get some funny looks becuase of his, er, um . . . unusual
appearance. But what he doesn't expect is – being taken for
granted by a right royal pain; having an unwanted baby
land on his doorstep; and becoming the villain of the piece
– when all he was trying to do is lend a helping hand.

ISBN 0 86327 514 1